About the Author

Peter was a teacher all his working life and is now a governor of a church school in Eastbourne where he lives with his wife. He loves living by the sea, reading novels and watching cricket. He has four grown up children and four grandchildren, two of whom live in Sydney. One of his teachers at school was William Golding, who wrote 'Lord of the Flies'.

Where's My Dad?

Peter Stone

Where's My Dad?

Olympia Publishers
London

www.olympiapublishers.com
OLYMPIA PAPERBACK EDITION

A CIP catalogue record for this title is
available from the British Library.

ISBN: 978-1-80074-085-3

This is a work of fiction.
Names, characters, places and incidents originate from the writer's
imagination. Any resemblance to actual persons, living or dead, is
purely coincidental.

First Published in 2022

Olympia Publishers
Tallis House
2 Tallis Street
London
EC4Y 0AB

Printed in Great Britain

Dedication

This book is dedicated to: Judy, my beautiful wife, my four children, Victoria, Kate, David and Richard, and my four grandchildren, Maddy, Joe, William and Toby.

Acknowledgements

I'd like to thank all the pupils at different schools over the years who've inspired me with their imaginations and love of stories: Berkhamsted, Ravenscroft, Stonar, Oakfield, Selwood, Wellsway, Berkley, St John's Meads, Beaumont House and Springmead.

Chapter One
The Dream

If only he would stand up, turn and smile at her. If only she could see his face. If only she could make him understand that she was there. His daughter, his only daughter, who loved him and missed him.

The man was always wearing a bright blue coat with the collar turned up and he sat on a bench halfway up the cliff path, looking out at a grey sea with a single yacht with a white sail. Chloe was always sitting just behind him on the grassy hill, unable to move or make a noise.

She opened her mouth to shout, "Dad! I'm here." But nothing came out.

She tried to bend down to pick up the smooth, white pebble at her feet. She would throw it gently at his back. Then he would know she was there. But she was paralysed, she couldn't move her hand.

It was getting dark, slowly at first, then more quickly. Then pitch black. She could stand! She could feel her way to the bench. She crawled. She felt the back of the bench. Empty. No one there. As always, the man had gone.

The Wakening

As always, she woke from the dream sobbing, hugging a wet and damaged teddy who had lost one arm and one eye over the years. The vision of her father faded, his unseen face slipping silently under the cruel waves in the grey sea. She would wake again to the reality of her tiny bedroom where it was just possible to close the door, if the bed was pushed right against the back wall, and where her precious dictionary lay on the wobbly table beside her bed, with the old lamp with no shade which provided the only uncertain light. The frayed, white curtains were tired and flimsy and provided little protection from the early morning sunshine in summer.

Sometimes, the dream would encourage Chloe to question her mother about her father, but she needed courage to ask because her mum usually seemed reluctant to have any sort of conversation about her dad. As Chloe grew older, she began to be more aware of her mother's mood swings, almost joking and happy one moment, then quiet and down in the dumps the next. Sometimes she dealt with Chloe's questions in a flat, almost bored, 'why are you bothering me again?' voice.

"He just disappeared when you were about two. I don't see how you could remember him. Best forget him anyway."

"No, I wasn't sorry. Happy to see him go."

"No, I don't miss him."

"No idea where he is."

"We've moved three times since then. He'd have no idea where we live."

"He sometimes drove a taxi but then there's nothing he wouldn't do to earn a few quid – not always legal, mind."

"I've told you before, love. I do not have a photograph. If I ever did have one, I'd have certainly thrown it away by now."

Eventually, her mum would become agitated and cross, determined to bring this interrogation to a close.

"Now, listen Chloe. These endless questions will not help you. We're better off without him. Just the two of us – against the world. That's you and me. And it's going to stay that way."

But once, just once, her mother had faltered at the question, "Do you miss him?" She had turned away from Chloe, reached for a tissue, blown her nose and grabbed a cigarette from the packet on the grubby table. She was briefly overcome but, inhaling the nasty smoke deeply, quickly returned to her sharp answers.

However, Chloe had seen enough to know there must still be some feeling between her parents, whatever the circumstances were.

She hated her mother smoking and had pleaded with her to stop.

"I don't smoke much, Chloe, only when I'm stressed. I need some pleasure in my life, you know."

Chloe wasn't sure how stress and pleasure went together with smoking but she knew when it was best not to challenge her mum. And this was one of those times.

Chapter Two
School's Closing

Chloe sometimes wished that her mum spent more time on her mobile phone, like Daisy's mum. When she went there for tea, she was happy to talk to the two girls and stare at her phone at the same time, endlessly scrolling down message after message, sometimes smiling, sometimes pulling a face. But, at least, Daisy could interrupt her without being moaned at. She supposed it was because her mum preferred the telly to the phone because she always said she didn't have many friends and received very few messages.

Sometimes, Chloe was desperate to talk to her mum but if she was engrossed in something on the telly, that could be very difficult. This particular Thursday evening Chloe knew she must, just must, speak to her mum. She saw the remote sitting invitingly on the edge of the coffee-stained arm of the sofa and, for a moment, but only a moment, thought of grabbing it and either switching it off or turning down the volume. Chloe had learnt to read her mother's moods. She didn't know why she was so often stressed, but she knew when she was.

As patiently as she could, Chloe waited for 'EastEnders' to finish before sitting cross-legged on the floor at her mother's slippered feet. This was a signal she wanted to say something and if her mum had finished her second glass of wine, she would sometimes smile and pat Chloe on the head.

"I was the only one who had their hand up."

"What are you talking about?"

"Me, I was the only one who said 'yes'."

"Yes, to what?"

"Mrs Tiler's question."

"Which was?"

"Put your hand up if anyone in your house smokes."

Mum shifted dangerously on the camping chair. Chloe edged back a little.

"What business is it of hers? I've seen that Barker woman – the one who helps in the class – having a fag in the playground when she thought no one was watching. Hypocrites the lot of them."

Chloe hated it when her mum was so nasty about grown-ups, particularly her teacher, Mrs Tiler, who she had grown to like and respect.

So, she carried on with the 'hands up' incident. "Daisy didn't put her hand up and her mum had a fag with her cup of tea when I went round their house."

"You should've been like Daisy and told a lie. I bet lots of those kids were too scared to put their hands up."

Chloe grew even bolder. "You told me never to tell a lie."

Silence. For once the telly had been turned off.

"Not a programme for you my little girl. You'll have to get ready for bed."

"But Mum, there's something I must tell you. It's important."

"Can't it wait 'til morning?"

"No, it'll be too late by then."

Deep sigh from the camping chair.

"Go on then. But hurry up. I don't want to miss this programme."

"If you had one of those box things, you could record

programmes and watch them when I'm in bed"

"I've told you before, Chloe, and I'll say it again slowly – we are not made of money. Now, get on with it, what's the problem?"

"You've heard about this virus thing that might kill lots of people all of a sudden?"

"Yes, of course, but it sounds like flu to me. Comes every winter."

"Well, Mrs Tiler says it's much worse than that, and to stop the virus spreading quickly, they're closing schools from next Monday. Have you heard about that, Mum?"

"Of course, I'm not completely ignorant, you know. I often watch the ten o'clock news when you're safely tucked up in bed, but I just don't go on about it all the time. So, I do know that some kids will still be able to be looked after at school. And you'll be one of them, my girl."

"Well, that's the thing, Mum. Some kids can go to school. If your mum or dad does something important like doctor or nurse, then they couldn't look after you at home 'cos they'd be needed in the hospital."

"Yeah, right, didn't know I was a doctor!"

"But even if you only work in Tesco's – 'cos it's helping get the food out – you could still have your kid looked after at school."

"Yeah, well, I don't work in Tesco's, do I?"

"And Mum?"

Reluctantly. "Yes."

Chloe knew she was in grave danger of upsetting her mum, who was always unhappy when Chloe quoted either Mrs Tiler or Mrs Barker, but she pressed on nevertheless.

"Mrs Barker took me into the corner and said to me, very

nicely, not bossy or anything, that if I was a child who got free school dinners, I'd be able to go to school during the virus thingy. I'd like that. Some of the dinners are quite nice."

A small explosion from her mum. "That woman should mind her own business. I know all about Free School Dinners and I do know that I'm not going to have that snooty lot at school looking down at me."

Silence. Chloe decided this was the moment.

"What is it you do Mum?"

Pause. Mum fumbled for another cigarette.

"I've told you before, Chloe. It's too complicated for a kid your age to understand."

"Well, maybe it'd be important enough to have me looked after at school. All you'd have to do is go into school and talk to Miss Yeats."

"What! That stuck-up head teacher of yours, no way. She told me to hear you read every day and make a record in some book of yours. I told her I often heard you read and that I thought it was the teacher's job to hear the kids read. She said it was everybody's job to… educate a child…"

Once again, Chloe had squirmed silently at her mum's attack on her head teacher but there was nothing she could say that would help the situation.

Suddenly Mum's mobile started singing some old Westlife song. She listened for a minute or so without speaking.

Then she spoke quietly but firmly.

"I've told you before. I'm not sure about tomorrow. And anyway, I've told you not to phone before half nine."

She ended the call and glared at Chloe, lit another cigarette and softened a bit.

"Are you telling me that on Monday you won't be going to

school?"

"That's right, Mum – unless you fix it with Miss Yeats and she knows what you do – something important with this virus thingy going on, that stops you from staying at home and looking after me."

"I've told you, I'm not seeing that Yeats woman."

Silence. Chloe spoke again, much more unsure of herself.

"Unless... unless, you can work at home. Liz's mother works in an office and because the office is closed, she'll be working at home."

Another small explosion from her mother. Chloe wasn't sure whether she was laughing or crying. The cigarette was making her cough and she stabbed it out angrily.

"You've no idea, have you Chloe? No idea at all how the world works. I could no more do my work at home than a... a... a train driver could."

She slowly recovered herself.

"Come here, give us a hug before you get ready for bed. I'm sorry I'm not the best mum in the world but we'll work something out. We'll come up with a plan at the weekend."

The hug smelt of cigarette and alcohol but for once, Chloe did not mind too much. She suddenly felt really, really tired. Despite everything, she loved her mum. Who else was there anyway? There was just the two of them against the world.

She fell asleep to the sound of a tinny Westlife on the phone.

Chapter Three
Laika

Saturday morning, nine o'clock – Chloe was waiting for her mother to get up. It could be some time yet.

Their flat was very small with only a brick wall to see from the living room window. The living room had the telly on an old chest, Mum's camping chair and an old grey sofa with lumpy cushions which was where Chloe usually sat. There was a small, green, plastic table at which they ate their meals (when their plates weren't perched on their laps). Sometimes Chloe was able to clear the ashtray from the table and do some written homework. She had a bedroom so small that she had to keep most of her clothes (not that there were many) in her mum's slightly bigger room. There was a shared bathroom and toilet on the landing which Chloe hated using. When they eventually moved into their own house (something Mum occasionally promised they would), their own bathroom was the one thing Chloe dreamt about as the greatest luxury life could offer. The kitchen was ridiculously tiny – a 'galley' kitchen her mum had called it once – with no room for more than one person at a time. It was separated from the sitting room by a curtain of red and blue beads.

Chloe discovered that a galley was a word used for small kitchens on boats. She was able to look the word up in one of the few books in the house, an old tattered copy of Chambers 'Compact Dictionary'; it gave three definitions, a long single-decked ship, propelled by sails and oars, a Greek or Roman warship, the kitchen on a ship. Chloe loved books and she just wished there were more things for her to read.

The only other book of much interest was an encyclopaedia, the sixth volume (L-N) of a series called 'A Fount of Knowledge for Enquiring Children'. Sadly, this was the only volume they had but Chloe devoured such knowledge as it had and picked up strange pieces of knowledge which sometimes impressed Mrs Tiler and which once amazed Miss Yeats, when she was taking assembly. She was talking about places in America and how names of mountains and rivers often came from ones the Indians had used.

"I don't suppose anyone knows what the word Mississippi meant to the Chippewa Indians." She looked around, not really expecting an answer. It struck Chloe that Miss Yeats often asked the children hard questions which no one could answer. To her surprise, and Chloe's considerable shock (she was not one to want to stand out at school), Chloe found herself putting her hand up.

"Well Chloe, do you know?" delivered in such a voice as to suspect that Chloe wouldn't have the faintest idea.

"It means large river," whispered Chloe.

"Speak up child! What did you say?"

"Large river, Miss Yeats."

"Goodness, gracious me!" said Miss Yeats. "House point to you, Chloe."

Chloe had tried to describe this miraculous event to her mum but without great success. It was another sign that her mother was more than usually stressed.

"Very nice, Chloe love, pass me the ashtray will you."

And so, Chloe survived as best she could on the encyclopaedia (L-N) and the Chambers Compact Dictionary. Her greatest joy – and sorrow – in the book of knowledge was an early entry about a dog called Laika, which is Russian for 'barker' or 'one who barks'. Laika was a stray mongrel found on the streets of Moscow who became one of the first animals in space and the first to orbit the earth in Sputnik 2 in November 1957. She was part-husky and part-terrier and looked very cute in the black and white photo, waiting for her great adventure in the space capsule. The great sorrow was that she probably only survived four days of the journey before dying in space when Sputnik's transmitters failed. Despite this sad ending – but Chloe often imagined the heroic dog parachuting to Earth to be greeted by cheering crowds – Chloe knew that her first real dog would be called Laika.

She couldn't decide whether it was a glamorous life that Laika had lived or whether it was just a cruel tragedy. She supposed it was what Mrs Tiler called a 'moral dilemma'. If a test of some cruelty to a dog could result in a child's life being saved from some dreadful disease, could it be justified? She liked the word 'justified'. The Chambers dictionary said it meant 'to prove something was fair or reasonable'. Could it be 'justified', she wondered, if she kept throwing away Mum's fags to save her life? That wouldn't work, though, would it? Her mum would just get super-angry.

Chloe loved those class discussions, even though she found it hard to 'speak up'. Mrs Tiler had got them to think about fox hunting – a fox was a pest and killed chickens mercilessly. Could we justify (that word again) in dressing up in funny clothes, blowing trumpets and chasing it over wet fields before the hounds rip it apart. Wouldn't it be fairer just to shoot them?

Many of Chloe's classmates didn't like these discussions. They were happier sitting in front of the computer doing

'Mathletics' or imagining they were the seventh wife of Henry VIII being crowned Queen. Chloe once told Daisy what nasty things had happened to some of Henry's wives. Daisy just said, "Don't be so horrible."

Chloe didn't have any really close friends at school. She had been to Daisy's house for tea but when it became clear that there'd be no return invitation, things rather cooled off. Some of her classmates ignored her as someone with nothing of any interest to recommend her – no mobile phone, no stylish clothes on a 'mufti' day, no stories of holidays in Disneyland, no pony or dog at home, no father with an important job. They didn't bully her, they just left her alone.

Once a week they had creative writing in groups with a visiting teacher called Mr Simons; he made silly jokes and made the children feel relaxed but he was quite demanding when he showed them how they could improve their writing. She was on a table with just two boys: Ben, who was small and wiry and always taking off the very strong glasses he wore, to rub them with an increasingly dirty handkerchief and Ned, who was athletic and popular and seemed to be good at everything. The boys did speak to Chloe during the group lessons but never at any other time. Still, she looked forward to these sessions and grew ever more confident in writing her own descriptions and poems. If only she had more books to read at home.

That Saturday morning, Mum finally emerged about half past ten.

"Be a love, Chloe, and nip to the SuperLocal and get a sliced loaf and some milk please." She hesitated. "And you know Mrs Martin, don't you?"

I certainly do, thought Chloe. Weird, elderly lady resembling a witch.

"Well, if she serves you and nobody's watching, just say two packets of the usual for my mum."

Chloe hated buying cigarettes for her mum. She knew it was illegal for her to buy them. She also knew that one packet would cost about ten pounds. All that money up in smoke!

"All right," muttered Chloe reluctantly. "You know it's illegal, don't you, Mum?"

Her mother said nothing but handed over a twenty-pound note.

Chloe wasn't sure whether or not her mum had realised this wouldn't be enough.

"I'll need more than that if I'm able to get the fags."

Once again, her mother remained silent but dug out her purse from her jeans pocket and slapped five one-pound coins on the table.

"And hurry up, there's a dear daughter. Be nice to your old mum what loves you."

Her mum seemed in a better mood this morning.

Chloe slipped quietly down the long, dark, dirty stairwell to the street outside. The brightness of the sun and the brilliant blue of the sky surprised her at first, then delighted her. She took a deep breath and silently asked God for help. She often said a prayer for help, though it never seemed to work. She remembered that Miss Yates once said in assembly that God always answered your prayers, but not straight away and definitely not always in the way you would like. She wasn't sure what to pray for; it was just everything really. She wanted Mum to stop drinking and smoking and be more – what was the word? – reliable. She wanted a much nicer house with a proper bathroom and a big garden. She wanted friends she could ask round for tea – and most of all, she wanted a dog.

That Saturday morning, outside SuperLocal on Seaway, whining pathetically and tied to the bike rack with a piece of flimsy and tired-looking string, was a dog. A sad-looking, brown and white dog, cowering and constantly scratching itself, its tail tucked between its hind legs. Was it a Jack Russell Terrier? Perhaps. Chloe knew better than to approach and stroke an unhappy dog but she fell in love with her instantly. This was Laika, the dog she was destined to own. Having been into the depressing shop to buy the milk and bread (fortunately no Mrs Martin), she decided to loiter outside a few minutes to see if she could find out who owned 'her' dog. She knew this was a crazy way to think but she'd said her prayer to God and was prepared to wait. The dog whimpered and whined and Chloe pretended to read the small ads in the grubby shop window. She was growing anxious; her mum would be angry if she was much longer.

Suddenly, to her amazement, her classmate Ben emerged from the shop and started to grapple with the clumsy knot he'd tied to keep the dog from running away.

"Hello, Ben," Chloe spoke nervously.

Startled, Ben turned round slowly. "Oh, hi Chloe. What you doing here?"

"Bit of shopping for Mum."

"Me too," said Ben. "Been landed with this flea-ridden dog too."

He stopped to find his filthy handkerchief and started to rub his glasses.

"Is it your mum's dog, then?"

"Oh no, it belongs to my uncle. He lives on his own and often goes away for work for days at a time. So, we get lumbered. My uncle doesn't look after her properly though. We do our best but it doesn't last. He won't give her up though. We've said we'll have her, but he always says no."

Chloe hesitated again. She wasn't sure if she wanted to be drawn into something that would end in tears. But she couldn't help herself.

"What's her name?"

"Lizzie."

Well, at least it started with an L.

"I've gotta go," said Ben.

"Are you going to school next week?" asked Chloe.

"No, my mum's at home."

"See you later, Chloe."

"Bye Ben, bye, Lizzie!"

Chapter Four
Life is Full of Surprises

When Chloe entered the flat a few minutes later, the living room was empty. She'd expected her mum to be having a 'coffee, a fag and a bicky' whilst reading a copy of 'The Metro' – if she'd been able to grab one when the bus was stopped outside their building. From the occasional muffled sound, Chloe realised she was in her bedroom. Not that her mum was ever very noisy in her room; she seemed to save all her annoying habits for the living room and her time with Chloe. She called the bedroom 'my one quiet place – do not disturb'.

Chloe took the risk of standing right up to the door with her ear pressed against it. She listened as hard as she could. Sometimes her mum would go in there to make a phone call but Chloe could never make sense of those one-sided conversations. Her mum spoke very fast and used some words which Chloe could not understand. But this was unexpected. Could this really be happening? It sounded as if her mum was crying, sobbing uncontrollably. She hardly ever saw her mum cry; she shouted quite a lot and occasionally screamed in rage. But crying? Hardly ever. Losing complete control? Never.

Time passed slowly. Chloe moved away from the door and sat on the sofa staring blankly at the scratched wallpaper with the picture of the Beachy Head lighthouse, thinking, wondering, feeling sorry for herself. She tried to say a prayer but nothing would come. If only there was a dog to cuddle. Even a sad and sorry-looking specimen like Lizzie – maybe not even but especially, a sad and sorry-looking specimen like Lizzie. She could give her all the love she'd been deprived of.

Finally, the door opened slowly and her mother crept out, red-eyed and clutching a letter.

"Mum, Mum, what's the matter?"

Her mother came and sat beside her on the sofa and put her arm round Chloe's shoulder, comforting, soothing.

"It's... it's... it's this letter. It's come out of the blue, it's a bit of a shock. I'll be all right in a minute, I'll calm down. Don't worry my love."

"Can I see the letter?"

Her mum panicked. "No, no, never, never!"

"But why not, Mum? Why not? It's made you really upset."

"It'll be all right in a minute, when I've had a chance to think about it all. You don't need to worry your little cotton socks about it. It's not going to change anything."

Her mum was being unusually affectionate. But Chloe knew she could not push her to explain the letter. Her best chance of trying to understand what was going on was to be loving and helpful. She'd never seen her mum so... so... what was that word Mrs Tiler used to explain the state of an unwanted dog thrown out of a car on a motorway – so...vulnerable! Yes, that was it. Vulnerable.

"Sorry, Mum, but Mrs Martin wasn't serving in the shop, so I couldn't get your cigarettes."

"Don't worry," said her mum. "I've been smoking too much lately. Ought to cut down. No point in smoking myself to death – not with a lovely daughter to look after."

Chloe was amazed. Her mother only ever talked like that if it was late in the evening and she'd drunk a lot from the bottle of red wine.

"And," her mum went on, "it's time we had some lunch. Beans on toast with cheese on top and chocolate ice cream from the freezer to follow."

Chloe couldn't remember when she had last felt so happy. But how could it be that a letter, that had made her mum howl with tears, be the start of this amazing change in her?

In the evening after they'd watched a game show on telly together and eaten their take-away fish and chips, Mum sprang another surprise.

"I've been thinking about Monday. You can't go to school, right?"

"Right."

"This is what we'll do. First, tomorrow we'll go to Smith's and buy you some of those school workbooks and an exercise book and things to write with. Then we'll come home and draw up a timetable for the week."

Was this woman really her mother? How had this change come about?

"Then we'll buy you a cheap pay-as-you-go phone. You'll be here on your own. Can't really go out, can you? Not allowed. But if there's an emergency, you can contact me on my mobile. Only if it's a real crisis mind!"

Chloe opened her mouth to speak but nothing came out.

"Could be boring stuck here on your own. If I'm back in time on Monday, we might get to the library so you can get your head stuck in a book. I know that'll keep you quiet for hours."

This must be a dream, Chloe thought. Soon I'll wake up and the room will be filled with smoke as usual.

"Course, you'll have to obey the rules. No going out! Got that? I should be home by half two each day."

Chloe opened her mouth and this time she did get the words out.

"Love you, Mum."

"I love you too, pet. Now get to bed."

Chapter Five
Monday Morning

Sunday had gone quite well, but not perfectly. No problem with the old SATs papers in Smiths and Chloe had persuaded her mum to buy her a sketch pad and some felt tips as well. The proposed trip to the library for today had not gone well, as Mum had no idea where the library cards were, or even whether they were still in date.

Still, continuing to behave like the new 'fairy godmother' mother she had become, she gave Chloe five pounds and said – if she was very, very careful – she could leave the flat for just a few minutes and run the short distance to the second-hand book shop down the road to choose some books and buy herself something for lunch from SuperLocal. "Got to keep you occupied somehow."

Chloe had been so excited she had let herself out of the flat as soon as she could after her mother had left for 'work' (whatever that might be) and made her way to the shop along the strangely deserted pavement. She passed the piles of aging books covered in a tarpaulin to find the blinds down with no sign of life. The sign announced that it was closed on Mondays. It should open on Tuesday at 10 a.m. but, looking around at the quiet street and the other closed shops, Chloe doubted that.

Deciding to spend some of the five pounds on her lunch, she went into SuperLocal to buy a 'meal deal' – a packet of crisps, a cheese roll and a bottle of coke. She was stuffing them into an old plastic bag she always carried in her pocket when she saw

Ben coming into the shop. He grinned at her.

"Oh, hi Chloe, what you up to?"

"Not much, just hanging around."

"I don't suppose you could do us a favour," said Ben, absent-mindedly rubbing his glasses with the handkerchief that looked like the same one she'd seen last time – but now even grubbier.

"Depends," said Chloe, not wanting to commit herself.

"Take Lizzie for a walk in the park. Mum's busy and she's given me some errands to do and Lizzie's no help at all. She won't be any trouble."

Chloe's mind was racing. There was no reason why she shouldn't – indeed there was every reason why she should. Taking a dog for a walk in the park! What could be better? Mum wouldn't know. There's no way she'd find out. She didn't seem to speak to any of the neighbours.

"Okay then. I'll do it."

"Thanks. Give it an hour and then drop her back at our house. Number 88, just down there by the zebra crossing. Lots of different flats. Just open the big door and ours is on the ground floor, first one on the right – 1a. Knock as hard as you can."

And then Ben was gone, not even stopping to buy anything. Nothing else said. No other instructions.

Sure enough, there she was, Lizzie, tied up with the same piece of horrible, dirty string. As a collar it was hopeless and probably hurt the poor dog. Chloe managed to untie it quite easily and she moved her hand uncertainly towards Lizzie's back, hoping to stroke her. The dog growled. Chloe tried again. The dog growled again, though a little less fiercely. Third time lucky. Lizzie allowed her to hold her hand there just for a couple of seconds.

And so it was that Chloe and Lizzie began their stop-start

walk to the park. Lizzie wanted to sniff every lamppost and tree they passed. Fortunately, there were no other dogs about, as Chloe wasn't sure how her new 'pet' would react to another dog. She was also worried that the string might break. She had no doubt that Lizzie would run off at great speed. She imagined herself standing there shouting helplessly, 'Lizzie, Lizzie, come here!' – as the dog vanished behind the rubbish bins beside the deserted tennis courts.

The park was strangely deserted. Chloe realised that this was probably because of this virus thingy – people had been told to stay indoors. She sat on a bench and managed to persuade the reluctant Lizzie to sit there for a moment. She could see a man in a black, leather jacket exercising a large Alsatian on the other side of the football pitch. Both the dog and its owner stopped for a moment and looked in Chloe's direction. For a horrible moment, Chloe thought they would change direction and come over to her but to her great relief, the owner tugged at the dog's lead and they disappeared round the old cricket pavilion.

Chloe didn't own a watch but she reckoned that about an hour had passed. She'd loved the time she'd spent with Lizzie but it had been a big responsibility and Chloe had been terrified she would lose the dog. She found number 88 without any trouble, and to her surprise, found that the old, scratched front door opened easily enough. Following Ben's instructions, she knocked as hard as she could.

No answer. She examined the door to 1a. It needed painting. No proper knocker, no bell. She banged again. Complete silence. Lizzie pulled on the string and scratched at the door.

Suddenly the door on the opposite side of the hallway opened and an elderly woman wearing a large, orange, Sainsbury's apron shouted at Chloe.

"You're wastin' your time. They've gone."

"Gone! Gone where?

"Dunno. She said somethin' about going off to 'er daughter's for a bit because of the virus. She and that boy of hers, whatever he's called."

"Ben, he's called Ben. But they can't have gone! I've got their dog."

"Glad to be rid of 'im I should think. Poor skinny thing. Needs a proper meal or puttin' down if you ask me."

Chloe could not believe that Ben's Mum and he had just run away, leaving her with the dog who was continuing to whine and scratch at the door.

Chloe was having to think fast.

"Ben said there was an uncle who really owned her."

The old woman in the orange apron drew a deep breath.

"That waster! You'll be lucky to find him."

"Do you know where he lives?"

"As a matter of fact, I do. When 'e's there. He's 'ardly ever there, mind."

The old lady grinned at Chloe and smiled a wobbly smile.

"Could you make it worth my while?"

Chloe had no idea at all what she meant.

"You know what I mean. Reward for information received!"

Finally, it sank in. The old woman wanted to be paid for telling her where Ben's uncle lived. Chloe felt the tears welling up. If this day had gone to plan, she'd be sitting at home now, eating her lunch and reading the book she'd bought at the book shop. Instead, well instead, it was turning into a nightmare.

She felt in her pocket for the change from her 'meal deal'. There were two pound coins and a fifty pence piece. She offered the fifty pence. The old woman grabbed it angrily.

"That's not much is it? Mean little so-and-so ain't yer? Still, I'll tell yer. He has a room above that pub down the road, The Pirate's Treasure. Not far. They'll be really pleased to see you, I'm sure!"

And the old lady in the orange apron laughed and laughed and vanished behind her door with a slam – leaving Chloe fifty pence poorer and holding an increasingly miserable dog by that useless piece of string.

Her mum had once – only once – taken her into a pub for a fish and chip lunch which had been delicious. She supposed it had been more of a restaurant really. She had passed The Pirate's Treasure sometimes and that was something else. She'd peered through the windows and seen huge television screens showing football and some men pulling handles on fruit machines. Outside, people were standing up leaning against the wall and pulling on their cigarettes as if their lives depended on it.

Did she dare walk in there and ask? She didn't even know the man's name. She could hardly go up to the bar and say, "Excuse me. But is Ben's uncle in, do you know?"

As it was, the pub was very quiet and as she dithered at the door, she heard a lady's voice and felt a warm arm round her shoulder.

"What is it love? Are you looking for someone?"

The morning had all been too much for Chloe. She burst into tears.

The lady led her to a chair in the corner and sat her down.

"Would you like a glass of lemonade love?"

Such kindness only made her cry more.

"That would be lovely. Thank you."

The lady disappeared for a moment and came back with a beautifully cold glass of lemonade and a packet of cheese and onion crisps.

"Hope you like these?"

"My favourite."

Chloe was good at saying the right thing sometimes. The lady sat opposite her and Chloe had a chance to see her clearly for the first time. She was probably a bit older than her mum but she had very black eyebrows, big eyelashes and wore very red lipstick. There was also a strong smell of perfume coming from her, a little sweet but pleasant nevertheless. Chloe thought she was perfect.

"Come on then… what's your name love?"

"Chloe."

"Chloe eh, nice name. Well, tell me, Chloe, what were you doing at my door and why are you crying?"

Sitting on that comfy chair with this motherly, smiling woman opposite her, Chloe felt she could pour her heart out. And she did. Very quickly. Everything: her mum, the letter, the flat, her dad, her dreams, school, Mrs Tiler, Miss Yeats, Daisy, the dog, Lizzie, Laika, Ben, the horrible woman in the orange apron, her fear of coming into the pub.

"You're a remarkable girl, Chloe. You've got guts, I must say. Life's dealt you some hard cards but you're ready to fight back if you have to."

Nobody had ever said anything to her like that before. She'd always thought she was a bit of a 'scaredy cat'. But here was this beautiful lady sensing something about her which made her glow inside with pride.

"What's your name?" Chloe felt brave enough to ask.

"Sandra, my name's Sandra, and coming to say hello is Mike, my partner. We run this place together. Mike, this is Chloe, she's come in for a drink and a chat, and brought with her a dog we know quite well."

A tall, thin man in blue jeans with a moustache and surprisingly long hair startled Chloe by speaking in what her mum would have called a very 'posh' voice.

"Well, hello there, Chloe, delighted to make your acquaintance and," he paused, "to meet again this unfortunate specimen of the canine variety, Lizzie. She looks exhausted."

As indeed she did, sound asleep on the floor, whining and twitching a little as if disturbed by unpleasant dreams.

Of course, Chloe realised, they would know the dog, wouldn't they?

"Ben's uncle lives here, doesn't he?"

Sandra and Mike looked at one another. Mike took a big breath and then spoke.

"The fact is, Chloe, that Ben's Uncle Tony used to rent a room here but he doesn't any longer. He paid up on Saturday and said we'd never see him again. Strange man, never really looked you in the eye when he spoke. I asked him about the dog and he said Wendy would have it."

"Wendy?"

"Ben's Mum."

Sandra squeezed Chloe's hand. "So you see, Chloe, we're going to need some help looking after... Lizzie. Or do you think it should be Laika from now on?"

Once again Chloe felt her eyes swelling with tears.

"Oh, Laika, please let it be Laika!"

Mike winked at Sandra.

"There's one thing I did find in his room – amongst a pile of litter he hadn't bothered to dispose of properly. I'll go and get it. Don't run away."

"Finish your lemonade, Chloe. We'll have to get on soon I'm

afraid."

Mike returned with a brown, leather collar which he placed carefully on the table. He raised his voice and spoke like a judge or an important policeman. "All owners are required to have an identity tag for their dog, giving the pet's name and address. A telephone number is always helpful."

"Can't think why Ben ended up using that wretched piece of string," said Sandra, "when there was a nice collar just sitting there."

"No tag with name and address though."

"Strange man that Uncle Tony. A real loner I think."

Suddenly Chloe gave a little scream. She'd seen the time on the clock behind the bar.

"It's two o'clock! My mum'll kill me if I'm not back home. I'm sorry… I'm sorry…"

Sandra stood up and held out her hands towards Chloe who placed her hands in Sandra's.

"Now, listen, Chloe. You go home as fast as you can. Talk to your mum. See if you can persuade her to bring you along about half six this evening and we'll have a chat about how you can help with the dog. If your mum's on side it would make your life easier wouldn't it?"

"Certainly would."

"It would help us, too. Because of this virus we'll probably have to close up the pub for a bit. Without you, not sure what we would have done with Lizzie. Wouldn't want to have her put down because we couldn't give her the attention she needs. That wouldn't be very nice, would it?"

Sandra stared hard at Chloe as she said this.

"No… no… it would be too horrible."

Chloe felt close to tears again.

Lizzie had stirred at the mention of her name and briefly wagged her sorry tail on the floor.

"She'll need some decent dog food, Sandra, and a basket to sleep in."

Sandra gave Chloe a hug.

"Right, off you go, and make sure you get your mum to bring you along about half six."

And she gave Chloe a big grin and an enormous wink.

Chapter Six
Answered Prayers

Chloe ran home, praying under her breath as she ran, holding her uneaten lunch and fearing the worst – just this once, Mum was bound to be early.

"Please God, let me get home before Mum. Please God, let Mum be in a good mood. Please God, let me see Lizzie a lot. Please God make Lizzie well. Please God, make Lizzie's name be Laika. Please God, save us from the virus."

She raced up the stairs without stopping, fumbled for her key, said another prayer, counted three for luck, and burst into the living room.

Deserted. No sign of Mum. Still, it was only twenty past two. She slumped on the sofa and started her lunch, crisps first, then the cheese roll, washed down with the coke. It was no surprise to Chloe that Mum still hadn't come back by quarter to three. She decided to turn on the telly. You could never tell with her mum. You could never be sure how she would react. Sometimes she hardly noticed the telly was on, would give Chloe just a quick kiss and disappear into her bedroom. At other times she might glare at the screen. 'What you watching that rubbish for, my girl?' And without having the faintest idea about the programme Chloe was watching, she'd grab the remote and turn it off.

At times like this, Chloe might play some of the word games she'd made up with the dictionary. She'd open the book at a double page and look at the word on the top left-hand side – perhaps it might be 'manager'. Then she'd look at the word at the bottom of the right-hand page – it might be 'mantle'. Then she'd write down as many words she could think of that might come between those two in the alphabet and be on that double page. Once Chloe had written her own report about herself – just like a school report. One of the things she'd written was, 'Chloe is very good at entertaining herself.'

This Monday afternoon Mum came home at about three and seemed in a good mood.

"Had a good day, my girl?"

"Pretty good, Mum, thanks."

Well, it was amazing really: different, strange, exciting, unexpected. How much could she tell her mum, should she tell her mum? But one thing was for sure – she had to get her to the pub this evening.

"Did you get to the book shop?"

"No, it was closed."

"Shame. Probably won't open again while this virus is about. Still, I have a surprise for you. A book."

"Really, Mum, that's great."

"Now, don't get too excited. It's not modern, fairly old, actually. But you're a clever girl and you like reading and this will give you lots and lots of reading! That's for sure!"

From her bag, she produced an old blue copy of 'Great Expectations' by Charles Dickens.

"Thanks Mum," said Chloe, uncertainly. A pause.

"Where did you get it? I mean, it's great – but you've never given me anything like this before."

"Well, I have now sweetheart. So just enjoy it."

"But, Mum, I'd like to know where you got it."

"As my mum used to say, that's for me to know and you to find out. Or, in this case, not find out. It's a little secret, that's

39

all."

"Okay, Mum, thanks a lot."

Chloe took a deep breath.

"Now, I've got something to tell you, and something to ask you."

"Not sure I like the sound of this."

"Nothing to worry about, Mum…"

Chloe gave her mum an edited version of the events of the day. She told her how she'd ended up with the dog (not mentioning the nasty lady in the orange apron) and the visit to the pub. She kept thinking her mum was about to explode but she didn't. She just sat there, shaking her head and occasionally smiling.

"You should have phoned me when you got stuck with the dog and Ben and his mum had done a runner."

"I didn't like to worry you."

"Well, fair enough, I'd have been worried all right!"

"But Sandra, the lady in the pub, is lovely, really kind. And Mike's got a really posh voice but he seems very nice. Please, Mum, oh please. They said about half past six and you wouldn't want me to go on my own, would you?"

There was perhaps a silence of half a minute.

Finally, Mum spoke.

"Okay, Chloe, you win. I suppose it will make a change. But what am I going to wear?"

"That blue dress you wore to the parents' evening, that's nice."

"Not much choice really. But I tell you one thing, my girl. We are not going to end up with that dog. This flat's far too small and dogs cost a lot of money – endless food and vet's bills."

"Okay, Mum, all right, no worries, you're a star, a real star!"

It seemed a very strange thing for Chloe and her mum to be doing, walking along Seaway, hand in hand, on their way to the pub. Chloe could tell Mum was quite nervous. Chloe was excited but worried at the same time.

It was still light when they reached the door of the Pirate's Treasure and there was Sandra ready to greet them.

"Well, I know who you are. You're Chloe and I'd give you a hug but it's not really allowed at the moment, is it?"

"And you've got to be Chloe's mum. You're very welcome… mmm…"

"Kirsty, I'm Kirsty. Thank you for asking us. I hope Chloe wasn't a nuisance at lunchtime."

"Not at all Kirsty, no problem at all. It's lovely to meet you – and we're not just being kind. We're hoping your daughter will be able to help us out with a little dog walking. Can I get you a drink, Kirsty?"

Chloe looked at her mum and raised her eyebrows, wondering and worrying what would happen next. She had never seen her mum in a social situation such as this. Chloe knew her mum sometimes drank two glasses of wine when watching the telly and – what she called – 'unwinding after a hard day'. Not that she ever gave Chloe any clues as to what the nature of the 'hard day' might have been.

Chloe was amazed – and a little impressed by what happened next. She had never realised what a good actor her mum was. She suddenly became an embarrassed teenager.

"Well, I don't usually drink very much, it always goes straight to my head and then I behave in a silly way." She giggled. "A nice, cold, Coke would be lovely."

Chloe had no idea whether or not Sandra was fooled by this performance. Whatever, she kept a straight face.

"…Ah, here's my partner, Mike. Mike this is Kirsty."

"I'd shake your hand if it was allowed, but greetings all the same."

That posh voice again.

"Absolutely delighted to meet Chloe's lovely mum. Hadn't expected she'd be so young."

Chloe thought, this is ridiculous. But she knew she'd have to play along with these grown-ups if she was going to have some happy hours with Laika.

"So, Kirsty, a Coke for you, a Prosecco for Sandra, and a lemonade for you Chloe. Is that right?"

"Yes… yes please."

The next surprise was her mother making polite conversation. Chloe realised that she had spent very little time with her mum with other people. Because Dad was a 'mystery man' in disgrace of some kind, there was no question of getting to know any of his family. Her mum avoided neighbours and didn't mention other people at work. Chloe realised that she was an only child with a single mum who seemed to have no friends. The lockdown would make things even harder.

"Well," said Kirsty, "this is very nice I must say. We're not ones for gallivanting about. It's just Chloe and me, you see. We keep ourselves to ourselves mostly."

Mike had arrived with the drinks.

"Well, with this lockdown about to happen, I think we'll all be keeping ourselves to ourselves. We'll probably be closed within a couple of days. It's going to be hard, losing our livelihood for a time. The government's said they'll be helping people like us but, even if they do, there'll be a lot of forms to fill in and a long time to wait before there's money on the table."

Sandra pulled a face.

"Not in front of Chloe, Mike. Let's get down to the business in hand."

Three young men came into the pub, laughing and pushing each other.

"Sorry," said Mike, "I'll have to serve them."

"It looks as if it's going to be busy. I should have asked you to come earlier." Sandra was looking round anxiously at the customers coming in.

"I suppose they're worried they might not see the inside of a pub for a bit," said Kirsty, sipping her nice, cold Coke.

"Too right," said Sandra. "Sorry to rush, but here's what I think should happen. Mike's arranged for the dog to see a vet tomorrow. See if we can get her on a better diet and a proper exercise routine. We also need a proper collar. So, Chloe, if you come round Wednesday lunchtime, say about twelve thirty, we'll see where we are and you can take Laika for a walk."

"Laika!" shrieked Chloe.

"That's right, that'll be the name on the collar."

Sandra looked knowingly at Mike as if he knew what he was supposed to do next.

"Oh Kirsty, perhaps we'd better have your phone number – just to be on the safe side. You never know."

"Of course, Chloe's got her own number as well. You might as well have both."

Chapter Seven
The Discovery

Life was certainly different at the moment. Chloe was usually wide awake by seven o'clock but the following morning, she was woken by her mum banging on the bedroom door.

"Wake up, sleepy head. No good you going drinking in pubs if you can't get up the following morning!"

Chloe yawned. "Sorry Mum."

"Nothing to be sorry for. Have a good day and don't go far. No dog for you, today, remember. See you this afternoon."

Chloe walked into the living room. This was a strange feeling. Mum gone to work in a good mood. No school. Cereal packet, bowl, spoon and bottle of milk on the table all ready for her. Her copy of 'Great Expectations' on the table beside the spoon.

She sat down to her cereal, taking her time, pouring the milk slowly. She had to admit that she did feel just a bit sorry for herself. Life was definitely more interesting than usual – and her mum was being really lovely to her. She'd also learned that her mother had quite another side to her, the one she'd revealed at the pub the previous evening. She'd obviously enjoyed her 'play acting'. As far as she could tell, she'd given up smoking and drinking as well, or at least cut down. Chloe had a big book to read, however hard it might be. She had a dog called Laika to take out for walks. And yet she was rather lonely. It was unusual for her to be in the flat by herself; her mum was usually there after school and at weekends. She missed school, too. Although she didn't really have any proper friends, she was sometimes included in games and no one bullied her any more. She was left alone to enjoy the lessons and sometimes chat to Mrs Tiler or Mrs Baker in the playground. There was Mr Simons' writing lesson to look forward to as well.

After breakfast, she decided to sit on the sofa and make a start on 'Great Expectations', or at least to 'get the feel' of it. She opened the book and gave it a good sniff. She loved the smell of new books but this was anything but new. It had a musty smell, as if it had been locked away in a dark cupboard under a dusty carpet for a hundred years. Mrs Tiler had taught her to look at the first few pages of a book to see the year when it was published. This edition had been first published in 1868 – an amazing one hundred and fifty-two years ago. It had very small print, was about three hundred and fifty pages long and had fifty-nine chapters. Chloe had looked at the number before the final chapter. It said LIX – which she knew was fifty-nine in Roman numerals, something else Mrs Tiler had taught her.

Settling down to the first chapter and feeling pleased at having managed the first page, she turned over to find something stuck between the next two pages. Sliding it out very carefully, she realised it was a postcard, written some time ago by the slightly faded look of it. On the front was a black and white picture of Seabourne Pier. Turning over, she was able to read the message:

Seabourne 21.3.82

Helen, my love. Weather here – wish you were lovely. Old jokes best, eh? Seriously, miss you so much my darling. Mother being very difficult. Far too cold for her. Should have stayed at home. I fear we may be sent to Falklands any day. Will you marry me? Much love Sid xxx

The address on the front was:

Miss Helen Farnes

23 Myrtle Avenue

Guildford

Surrey

And that was that. Chloe's mind was racing, so many questions, so many unknowns. Setting aside 'Great Expectations', she found a piece of paper and started what Mrs Tiler would have called a 'Brainwave Investigation':

When was this written? 1982.

Where was it written? Seabourne (not necessarily).

How long ago is this? 38.

Who wrote it? Sid.

Who was it sent to? Helen.

How old do you think Helen might have been? 20-25? (Guessing!).

If she were still alive, how old would she be now? 58-63?

How old would Sid have been? Bit older than Helen? 23-28? (More guessing!).

If he were still alive, how old would he be now? 61-66.

Any surnames? Helen's on the address.

Any addresses? One on the front. Helen's.

Why was it sent? Keen to be in touch.

Tone of greeting: Bit jokey, bit of a moan about Mother, and *MARRIAGE PROPOSAL!*

Marriage proposal: Why write it on a postcard for everyone to see?

Had he proposed to her before? Was he serious?

Chloe was really excited. This would call for great detective work. She remembered watching a film with her mum on telly about Miss Marple, an old lady who solved a difficult case. Well, she was an old lady, Chloe was a young woman. Perhaps she could solve this one. But what exactly was she trying to solve? She thought about that for a moment. It was quite simple really. Did they ever get married? Are they still alive? She turned the card over to the side where the address was. There was the stamp with the Queen's head on it.

Then something struck her – her first piece of real detective work.

The postcard had not been – what was the word when they stamped it to show it had been paid for and posted – franked. 'Franked' yes, that was the word. The card had never been sent! Had it been delivered by Sid in person? Or had it never been sent? Had Sid ever proposed to her before? What did she say? Why would he be going to the Falklands? They were islands, weren't they? Where were they? Why would Sid want to go there?

And then she saw something else. In very small print at the bottom of the postcard it said, 'Purchased at the Prince Albert Hotel, Seabourne.'

So many questions. So much to find out. How exciting.

Where was this hotel? Was it still called that? Did it still exist?

So that was a plan for today. Find out about the hotel. Fetch Laika. Take a walk and investigate!

Chapter Eight
The Hotel

"Sandra, I'm sorry to be a nuisance, but do you have a computer?"

"My, you're coming out of your shell I must say."

Chloe blushed and then spoke very fast, the words tumbling out one after the other. "I'm sorry, it's just that I've found an old postcard in a book by Charles Dickens and I want to find out if the Prince Albert is still a hotel in Seabourne."

"Well, well," came Mike's posh voice. "That's very interesting. Are you Miss Marple or what?"

"Oh no, I'm not as clever as her."

"Nor as old! And we thought the first item you'd require would be one dog by the name of Laika."

"But I do, I do. It's just that I need to find out about the hotel so I can take Laika there on our walk."

"And what would be the name of the hotel?"

"It's called The Prince Albert."

"Well, I'll have a look on my phone."

One day, thought Chloe, I'll have a phone like that and I'll be able to look things up without having to ask other people.

Mike moved his fingers across his screen, pulled a face and then spoke.

"No luck, I'm afraid. But I'll see if there used to be one. Popular name for the Victorians."

Another pause while fingers flashed across the screen.

"Here we are… Prince Albert. Changed its name in 1997 –

now called 'Jubilee Hotel'."

Chloe almost jumped up and down with excitement. "Where is it now?"

"Let's see. It's on Edmund Street, narrow street that runs down to the sea near the pier. Here, I'll show you on Google Maps."

They peered at the screen together.

"There you are, and there's your route, seventeen-minute walk. Think you can find it?"

"Yes, thank you. Mum and I used to do a lot of walking round the neighbourhood. Mum said that if you lived near the sea, you should make sure you go to see it every day."

"Do you?"

"No, we don't. Mum's not so keen on going for walks now."

At that moment, Sandra swept into the bar with the dog which looked much the same as yesterday – perhaps not quite so scruffy. And was that a little wag of its tail? She certainly had a smart, new, brown, leather lead with a silver tag attached. Chloe bent down to read it.

"It says Laika! Oh thank you, thank you."

"You're all legal by the way, tag and phone numbers and everything."

"You're so kind, thank you."

"You're very welcome. She looks ready for a walk. Off you go! Have a great time."

Just as they were passing through the door, Sandra called them back.

"No wait, wait. You'll need these; you've got to be a responsible dog owner, Chloe."

She was handed some little black bags and a small shovel.

"You know what they're for?"

49

Chloe blinked. She stuttered, "Yes, I do, I do, thank you."

Then they were off. Out into the wind and the sun, moving more quickly than Monday. Perhaps Laika had eaten one or two proper meals since then. She certainly seemed more alert and she was even more keen to stop and sniff everything that interested her: lamp posts, old bits of newspaper, even the shoes of an old man waiting for the bus. Chloe knew that dogs lived in a world of smell. How strange. She loved dogs but she wasn't sure she'd like to be one.

Suddenly, there was a growl; a large, black dog had slipped its lead and the owner was standing chatting idly to a beggar sitting in the doorway of the SuperLocal.

"Oi, Charlie! Come 'ere. At once!"

To Chloe's surprise, Charlie did go there, at once.

"Sorry about that," said the owner. "Big, black dog wouldn't hurt a fly really."

And then Laika began to bark ferociously at Charlie just to make the point that she'd been in charge all along.

They weren't far from the hotel now and Chloe was starting to feel nervous again. Perhaps it would be easier to be quite truthful; she'd done nothing wrong. She was interested, that was all. The people in the hotel might be pleased to do something a bit different; there certainly weren't many visitors about. That would be because of the virus thingy – which reminded her. She really must wash her hands more often. Not that her mum seemed that bothered.

Chloe was now talking to Laika most of the time when there was no one around to hear. "Here we are. Edmund Street. Quite narrow. Wouldn't get one of those big coaches down here, would we Laika? And what are you sniffing now you silly dog? It's only an old paper bag. Now behave yourself. Don't want you getting us thrown out. Might have to tie you up outside anyway. Right. Here we go. Here's the entrance."

The entrance hall was surprisingly small and quite dark. There was a reception desk covered in all those leaflets advertising the wonderful tourist attractions nearby. Behind the desk was a large painting of what appeared to be Seabourne of long ago, a street with horses and carriages with men in top hats and ladies in long dresses carrying parasols (thank you Mrs Tiler). There was a hand bell on the desk placed on a notice which read, "Ring for Assistance."

Chloe rang the bell uncertainly. Laika had found something of great interest to her in a waste paper basket standing just by the desk. At the moment when a tired-looking lady in a blue overall appeared behind the desk, the waste paper basket fell over revealing the remains of some sort of a pie in a packet which Laika was attacking with great glee.

"Oh dear," said Chloe. "I'm so sorry." She didn't know what else to say.

"Well," said the woman, "apart from your dog enjoying its lunch at our expense, what can I do for you?"

The woman had grey hair tied tightly in a bun and seemed to be wearing dark glasses, which was strange because the light in the hall was pretty gloomy.

"I'll try to clear up the mess," stuttered Chloe, "but I'd need a dustpan and brush or something…" She ran out of things to say as the woman just stared.

"I think you'd just better control your dog. I'll clear that mess up later."

She paused, before going on in an irritated tone.

"Now, what do you want? Presumably you don't want a room or a job. Far too young. Are you looking for someone? Most of our guests have left because of the coronavirus."

Chloe took a deep breath.

"I'm trying to get some information on someone who might have stayed here in 1982."

The woman started to laugh. She paused to catch her breath.

"That's really very funny, you know. Girl turns up off the street with a mangy dog wanting to know something about someone who might have stayed here in 1982. Which, according to me, is thirty-eight years ago. Is this some sort of practical joke?"

"Oh no, it's not a joke. You see I was given this old copy of 'Great Expectations' and in it was a postcard and..."

"I'm going to stop you there, young lady. I've no time to hear this story of yours, I'm far too busy. And anyway, I don't know anything about the past here. I've only been here six months."

"Aren't there any old registers or something like that?" asked Chloe.

"Who's the smart one then?" the woman said. "Now listen to me, there's nothing I can do. But," she went on in a slightly changed tone, "the owner works on Thursdays and Fridays in the mornings and he might be able to help you. What's your name by the way?"

"Chloe."

"Okay then, Chloe, you take yourself and that dog of yours out of here now and I'll leave a note to Mr Cooper to say you might be in tomorrow or Friday to ask some questions."

"Is he nice?"

"What kind of a question is that? He's nice enough."

She grinned for the first time and put on a silly monster voice. "Nicer than me anyway."

"Thank you very much Mrs... Mrs... mm?"

"Miss Harper."

"Thank you, Miss Harper."

On the way out, Chloe noticed the bookcase standing just by the desk. What she saw was a great surprise. As soon as she and Laika were out of the door, Chloe resumed her constant chatter with Laika, who, when not sniffing, seemed to be listening to what Chloe was saying.

"But don't you think that's odd Laika? Or do you think it's just coincidence? I suppose those editions of Dickens must be quite common, but it's a bit of a coincidence, isn't it? Don't suppose you've read much Dickens, have you Laika?"

Chloe stopped talking as a young woman talking on her phone swept past, without so much as a glance at the girl with the dog.

"Miss Harper called you 'mangy'. That wasn't very nice was it? I think it means you're scruffy and dirty, with some kind of nasty disease. I hope that didn't upset you."

Chloe stopped as they reached the main road and there were more people about. She had to pull Laika out of the way of a speeding cyclist.

"Oi, look out maniac!" someone shouted.

The cyclist had vanished, probably never heard a thing.

Chloe felt she must stop talking to Laika as if she were a real person. She knew it was partly because she didn't have a proper close friend but that didn't make it right. Perhaps, she should just concentrate on sounding soothing and loving.

"We'll soon get rid of that mangy look, Laika. You wait and see. I love you and Mike and Sandra love you too."

They quickly reached the pub. The door was closed, and to Chloe's surprise, there was a typed notice pinned to the door. She read it slowly, her mouth falling open as she did so:

CLOSURE OF THE PIRATE'S TREASURE INN.

Because of the current crisis, along with many other businesses, we have made the difficult decision to close the pub with immediate effect.

We offer our apologies to our lovely loyal customers.

Signed: *S. Haddon. M. Carter-Brown*

Chloe rang the bell. No answer. She banged on the window. No answer. The curtains were closed. She went to the door by the side of the building which led to the pub's delivery area. It was locked. She looked at the notice again. No forwarding address. No telephone number.

Chloe was stunned. All this could only mean one thing. Mike and Sandra had run away. For the second time in three days, Chloe had taken Laika for a walk only to find that she'd been abandoned, betrayed. She looked down at her dog – yes, it was her dog now, surely – patted her head and tried to be cheerful. Not easy.

For a moment Chloe panicked. This was hopeless. Why not take off the tag and just let the dog loose in the park? Let someone else sort it out. Her mum would go mad if Chloe came back with the dog.

But she wasn't 'the dog' was she? She was Laika, a special dog who'd somehow become her dog, Chloe's dog. She'd just have to be brave – for Laika's sake.

Then she noticed the phone numbers on Laika's tag. They were her mum's and hers. Why had Sandra and Mike been so horrible when they had just been so nice? Why had they gone to such trouble to give Laika a good home? None of it made much sense.

What was her mother going to say?

Chapter Nine
The Dog's Home

When her mum came home and found Laika sitting in a slightly damp cardboard box which Chloe had found outside SuperLocal, she was not at all pleased. In fact, she was steaming with rage.

"This is too much, Chloe, just too much! I cannot, will not, have that dog in the flat. It's not your dog, we can't afford to keep it, we can't afford the vet's bills, we can't afford the food, it's not fair on a dog to be cooped up here, we're not... and this is a very big 'and'... even allowed to have pets under the terms of our lease."

For a moment, Chloe thought her mum was going to cry. She was shaking so much, trembling with anger.

Chloe went over to her and put her arms round her.

"Just let me explain, Mum, please. It's not my fault."

"What do you mean, 'it's not your fault'?"

"Mum, sit down please. Shall I make you a cup of tea?"

"No, no, don't worry about the tea. Just explain – before I run away to leave you and that wretched dog living here on your own!"

Chloe was an honest girl, well usually anyway. But she knew she could not yet tell Mum about the postcard and the hotel. For the time being, she could leave out that bit of the story without telling a lie. She had an uneasy feeling about those blue Dickens' books, she couldn't explain it to herself, not yet. But first she must explain about Sandra and Mike and the pub and the notice on the door and the phone numbers. That was why Laika was sitting in that nasty cardboard box in the flat, starting to whine and whimper. She was probably getting very hungry. Chloe had no idea whether she'd been fed in the morning.

So, she told her mum about collecting Laika, how nice Sandra and Mike had been (just like the evening before), about Laika's smart new lead and tag, about taking the dog for a walk and returning to the pub to find the notice. What else could she have done? She had to bring Laika home. She couldn't just abandon her in the street. She tried to explain to her mum how difficult it had been, but it was hard to get the words right.

"I... I... wanted to cry, I wanted the... gr-ground to swallow me up, I n-needed you to be there, to tell me what to do and to say it will all be all right."

There was a pause. Chloe's mum was looking at her, as if she was looking at a picture in a gallery trying to decide what it was all about. Then she stepped forward and put her arms around her daughter, hugging her tightly, and whispering in her ear, "There, there, my love, don't cry, it will be all right in the end, you'll see."

Then, they sat together on the sofa holding hands, saying nothing and looking at the dog in the box. The dog in the box was looking at them too. Chloe wondered what she might be thinking, but it was hard to imagine doggy thoughts. Perhaps she's wondering where her next meal's coming from. What Laika did, in fact, was to try to scramble out of the box, and in doing so, made the box collapse into a damp heap on the floor. Excited by her new freedom, she ran about the room sniffing at everything and even wagging her tail. And then, to Chloe's amazement, scrambled onto the sofa and managed to wedge herself between mother and daughter.

"Well, well, well," said her mum. "What can I say?"

And she started to laugh and laugh and laugh, and so did Chloe. It was a wonderful moment of joy, and one Chloe would never forget.

Then Mum suddenly stood up in a business-like way, brushing some doggy hairs from her skirt.

"Right, my girl, enough is enough. I think that's settled one thing. We've been lumbered with this animal and that's that. It's certainly never going to win the Cruft's Dog Show. For better, for worse, for richer or poorer and so on. And in our case, it's worse and not better and certainly poorer and not richer. So we need a plan, a realistic plan."

"Mum, Mum, I'm so sorry, it's just that…" Chloe tried to interrupt.

"Just hear me out my girl. It hurts me to say this but we're not due another landlord inspection 'til June, so we do have a bit of time." She paused and spoke more quickly. "In a minute, I'm going to SuperLocal and I'm going to find a better, stronger box and some dog food and biscuits. We've got a couple of old bowls which will be fine. Your job is to look after that dog and see it doesn't do any damage."

"Mum, mum, its name is Laika and it's a 'she', not an 'it'."

"Well, she may need to earn her promotion from 'it' to 'she' by good behaviour. We'll have to see." She paused again and put on her most serious of faces. "And Chloe, have no doubt. This is not going to be easy. It's a difficult time. I've got to work, you can't go to school, we're not supposed to have any pets in the flat – and… and Money Doesn't Grow On Trees! And… and… in the end we just might not be able to keep her. We'd have to take her to the RSPCA."

"Or have her put down…" said Chloe miserably.

"I'm off to the shop now," said her mum, closing the door firmly behind her.

Chapter Ten
Subterfuge and Surprise

Chloe was thinking hard. She needed to get out of the house to visit the hotel to see if Mr Cooper, the owner, was there. Miss Harper had given the impression that he might be a softer touch than she was. But perhaps she was only joking. Perhaps he would be angry at being disturbed by a little girl showing him some silly postcard written hundreds of years ago when the hotel wasn't even called by the name it is now.

But the first problem was reaching the hotel. Because of the lockdown there weren't so many people on the streets now and a girl on her own might make people wonder what she was doing. The police might see her and start asking questions. Why aren't you at school? Why aren't you at home? What's your name? How old are you? Where do you live?

Should she take Laika with her?

After much thought, she decided that taking Laika could make things worse, certainly in the hotel. She needed a 'subterfuge'. This was a word Mrs Tiler had taught the class on one of her 'Big Interesting Words' days. She explained that it was 'a trick or a deception' to get you out of a difficult situation. Chloe wasn't happy about lying and tricks and deception, but she thought that this was an occasion when one was needed. After all, no one would suffer because of it. She had been impressed by Mrs Tiler's story about Winston Churchill who had been Prime Minister during the war. Apparently, you're not allowed to call anyone 'a liar' in Parliament so he said that what another Member of Parliament had said was a 'terminological inexactitude'. Chloe thought this was funny and very clever – a pity she couldn't think of something equally brilliant.

After much thought, she came up with an idea which she thought was pretty feeble but was the best she could do. Not far from the hotel was the doctor's surgery which she and her mum belonged to. The doctor her mum liked to see was a lady doctor called Doctor Keith – which her mum used to say was quite funny, because really, you'd expect Doctor Keith to be a man and not a woman. Whatever – as Daisy would have said – Chloe found an envelope and wrote the name 'Dr Keith' on it. Then she sealed it. There was nothing inside. If she was stopped by the police, or any other busybody for that matter, she would show them the envelope with the doctor's name on it. If she was asked to open it to prove that her story was true, she would explain that she couldn't possibly do that because it was 'confidential' between her mum and the doctor. 'Confidential' was another word she liked. Mrs Tiler explained that if anybody had a problem, they could talk to her and what was said would remain 'confidential'. Nobody else would know what was said unless you said that she could pass it on.

Chloe hoped and prayed that no one would stop her and ask what she was doing. Still, she had a story which made sense and she had some evidence to prove it. She was ready to go.

Laika had been looking a little sleepy but as soon as she saw Chloe on the move, she jumped out of her box and stood by the door wagging her tail. She was already much livelier; the dog food was beginning to work its magic and Chloe's leaving her alone in the flat at this moment was not going to work. She loved this dog but she was beginning to see that it wasn't a toy you could pick up and put down just as you pleased. She needed a run in the park to work off some energy and to do her business.

So, that's what happened – out of the door, across the surprisingly quiet road and into the almost deserted park. And who should she see standing by the slide? Ben!

"Ben, what are you doing here?"

"What do you mean, Chloe? What am I doing here? I live just down the road, don't I? That's what I'm doing here? What are you doing here?"

"I'm taking this dog of yours for a walk."

She immediately regretted saying 'of yours'. But it was too late to withdraw it.

"Excuse me, Chloe. It's not my dog. Never has been. Did belong to my uncle, but he's done a runner."

He stopped to look at the dog's collar.

"And it looks like this dog is called Laika and belongs to these people with these phone numbers. Not my mum's number. I don't have a phone. Do you have a phone, Chloe?"

"None of your business, Ben."

"If you say so, Chloe. I'll see you later. Or maybe I won't."

"You tricked me, Ben."

"I don't think so, Chloe. Didn't know my mum was going to take us away for a couple of days. Or that my uncle was gonna scarper. Anyway, you've done all right haven't you? I could see you wanted that dog. And now you've got it. And, that other dog was called Lizzie, this dog's got another name. Laker or something."

"Laika actually." She paused. "Why are you being so horrible to me, Ben? After all, it was you who asked me to take the dog for a walk."

Chloe was surprised that she was able to speak to Ben like this, but things had changed in the last few days. Her mother seemed to have had a change of heart of some kind, she'd become a dog-owner, she'd dared to go into the pub on her own and she'd found the postcard and the hotel and spoken to the receptionist. Some of these things had been frightening, but they'd also been exciting.

Ben was surprised too. His face even turned a little red. He spoke more slowly in a deeper voice.

"It's my mum, Chloe. She told me to keep clear of you and the dog. 'Whatever you do', she said, 'don't get involved'. Yes, that's what she said, 'Don't get involved'."

"Well, you don't need to worry, Ben. No chance of us getting involved with you."

And with that, Chloe and Laika sped across the playing field as fast as the lead Chloe was grasping for dear life would allow.

Chapter Eleven
Back to The Jubilee

As Chloe closed the door to the flat, she pressed her ear against it and listened. She could hear a little whimpering, nothing too much, but definitely there. Then a little bark. Then some whining, then more whimpering. She stepped away and counted to fifty before listening again. She said a little prayer. Silence. She counted to twenty. Still silence. She thanked God, checked her bag with the copy of 'Great Expectations', the postcard and the doctor's 'letter'. Her mobile phone was in her pocket. Ready to go at last.

Seaway was strangely quiet for a Thursday morning at eleven o'clock. Some traffic, but not too much – mostly bin lorries and buses with nobody in them. The pavements were quiet too – apart from the odd cyclist who seemed to ignore the almost empty road, in preference to racing at high speed, past unsuspecting pedestrians. But Chloe was nervous, a girl on her own might look suspicious. What could she be up to? She held her bag even more tightly, trying to look like somebody on an important errand, not running but walking quite fast.

She reached the zebra crossing. Being careful to obey the code for crossing the road, she looked both ways and stepped out. Why had she not heard the police siren? Perhaps it had only just been switched on, perhaps the car had been going so fast it was upon her before she even knew it. For a brief moment, she was paralysed. She just stood there, frozen, unable to move either forwards or back. The car screeched to a halt just before the crossing. The passenger window was wound down. A policewoman shouted at Chloe.

"Get a move on, pet! We're in a hurry."

Chloe did get a move on but by the time she reached the opposite pavement, the police car had already sped away, siren blaring, towards the recreation ground. She realised she was trembling. She thought about turning round and going home but, after holding her breath and counting to twenty, she gripped her bag even more tightly and moved off towards Edmund Street and the Jubilee Hotel.

As she entered the narrow street and caught a glimpse of the hotel sign, she realised she was about to fall over a pair of legs in dirty, grey trousers. She stopped and walked off the pavement into the narrow street.

"Got some money for a cup of tea, love? I'm parched."

The voice was not unlike Mike's in the pub, surprisingly posh.

Chloe was taken aback. She'd often seen these people in the street but no one had ever spoken to her so directly before. She was embarrassed. She wasn't sure what to do. She didn't have her purse with her. She didn't want to walk on and not say anything. Who knows what he might do? Oh dear, this walk was full of dangers: the police car, the zebra crossing, and now this black man in the dirty, brown-grey trousers with an old baked beans tin at his side. She didn't want to just ignore him. She usually felt sorry for beggars. She and her mum knew what it was like to have very little money. But they always had enough for tea, milk and biscuits.

She stopped, turned towards him, and stuttered as she spoke.

"I'm sorry, I don't have any money. I'd like to help you but…"

63

Was that a mistake to say she'd like to help him? Probably. She looked at him properly for the first time: beard, long hair, but much younger than she'd expected.

"What you got in your bag, love?"

Without thinking she told him.

"A letter for the doctor, a copy of 'Great Expectations' and an old postcard."

He looked truly amazed.

"Well, strike me down, a copy of that great Dickens novel! Who'd have thought that? I wouldn't have guessed that if I'd sat here for a hundred years. Nor the other two things. Extraordinary, truly extraordinary!" He changed tone, spoke more seriously.

"What's your name, love?"

"I think I'd better be going," stammered Chloe. "My mum will be wondering where I've got to."

He stood up, looking quite different. He was tall and quite imposing.

"I'm sorry," he said in his educated voice, "shouldn't have startled you. I'm just an old drunk down on my luck. I used to teach at a university, English literature – can you believe that looking at me now?"

Chloe didn't know how to respond. She grasped her bag ever more tightly.

"I really must go."

He slumped down again, against the wall, dirty, brown trousers blocking the pavement.

"I do hope you get your money for the cup of tea."

"So do I love, so do I." His voice trailed away.

She didn't turn round but made straight for the entrance to the hotel. Her heart was racing as she passed the bookcase with the blue copies of Dickens; she needed a minute or two to compose herself before speaking to Mr Cooper. She even looked carefully at the titles of the books. There appeared to be only one copy of each book, so she reasoned that if there was a copy of 'Great Expectations' there, then it was much less likely that the one her mother had given her would have come from the hotel. But she couldn't find one: 'Oliver Twist', 'David Copperfield', 'A Christmas Carol', 'Bleak House'… but no 'Great Expectations'.

The police car and the beggar had made her nervous, less sure of herself than when she had set off leaving Laika alone in the flat. She just prayed that the dog was behaving herself and not wrecking the flat.

She seemed to be doing a lot of deep breathing and counting today. She hoped no one could see her. Perhaps the owner had a way of seeing people at the desk without being seen himself, one of those two-way mirror thingies. Anyway, regardless, she took some deep breaths and counted to fifty. Then she rang the bell. She felt a dip pit in her stomach.

Silence. A deep silence – unusual in these times: no music, no distant traffic, no shouting, no radio or television noise, no mobile phone ringing. She rang the bell again. Nothing. Then she noticed the sign behind the desk.

"No vacancies due to coronavirus. In emergency, phone 07700900537."

Well, there we are – one of Mrs Tiler's 'Big Words' – dilemma. Chloe was in a dilemma, should she phone that number and risk upsetting the owner for ever and ever and never finding out any more about the postcard? Or should she come back another day and try again? But then the notice would still be the same. The virus wouldn't have suddenly vanished in the night. She looked at it again and read out loud. You couldn't say that her quest was an 'emergency' could you? It might intrigue somebody on a dull day but you never knew.

Then it struck her. If the hotel was closed and you didn't want anyone to come in why wasn't there a notice on the front door? And why wasn't the door locked? Perhaps Miss Harper had told Mr Cooper about Chloe's visit and he was genuinely interested? Oh really, thought Chloe. That's ridiculous.

But, nevertheless, she tapped out the number.

07700900537.

It rang and it rang and it rang. Finally, a message:

"Hello, this is John Cooper. I'm sorry I can't speak to you right now. If you want to stay at The Jubilee, I'm afraid you can't because of the coronavirus. If you'd like to speak to me about something else, please leave your name and a short message with a number. Thank you. "

Chloe was bitterly disappointed. How stupid of her not to realise that Mr Cooper would hardly be hovering around the desk waiting for phantom guests. But, having got this far, she decided she'd leave a message in any case. She panicked when she thought of what might happen if he phoned when she was at home and her mum was there. The uneasy, deep pit in her stomach returned, but she carried on anyway, talking rather too quickly.

"Hello, Mr Cooper. My name is Chloe Hopper. I spoke to Miss Harper the other day about a postcard I found in an old book and she thought…"

"Well, hello there Chloe," came a deep voice from behind her. She turned round to see quite a round, fat, elderly man with a completely bald head. He was wearing old fashioned silver glasses which kept slipping down his nose. "How can I be of assistance?"

Chloe was very nervous and blurted out her story far too quickly.

"Slow down, just slow down. You sit on that chair over there and I'll sit on the sofa. Tell me your story again, slowly, very slowly, then you can give me the postcard to look at."

And that's what she did.

Mr Cooper spent some time studying the postcard, constantly pushing his glasses back onto his nose. It was very quiet in the hotel. For the first time, Chloe noticed a solid, brown grandfather clock in the corner. The ticking seemed very loud in the silence.

Seabourne 21.3.82

Helen, my love. Weather here – wish you were lovely. Old jokes best, eh? Seriously, miss you so much my darling. Mother being very difficult. Far too cold for her. Should have stayed at home. I fear we may be sent to Falklands any day. Will you marry me? Much love Sid xxx

The address on the front was:

Miss Helen Farnes, 23 Myrtle Avenue, Guildford, Surrey.

"Mr Cooper, can you see the very small writing at the bottom of the postcard?"

"I can see there's something there, my dear, but it's far too small for me to read. I've a magnifying glass in the office, I'll go and fetch it."

"I'll fetch it for you Mr Cooper, I know where it is."

Chloe was surprised to see a young man with a confident air, dark haired, highly-polished black shoes and a white shirt, standing there perfectly still and quiet, almost unnoticeable.

"Oh Chloe, this is Tom, helpful lad, does some odd jobs for me now again. How you getting on with the cellar, Tom?"

"Oh, fine, Mr Cooper, just fine. Good thing I don't drink,

though. Lots of bottles of wine down there."

And then Tom vanished as suddenly as he had appeared.

He returned with a large, bronze magnifying glass which he handed over to Mr Cooper, who pressed it to his right eye once he'd removed his glasses.

"Ah yes, ah yes, very good, very good. It says 'Purchased at the Prince Albert Hotel, Seabourne.' Which we now know to be The Jubilee Hotel Seabourne. Changed its name in 1997, one hundred years after Queen Victoria's diamond jubilee. The very year in which I took charge. I felt that Prince Albert, splendid man though he was and much loved and mourned by the dear queen, made the place sound rather old-fashioned. Not the name for the twenty-first century. Not that I'm a man of the twenty-first century either." He laughed quietly at what he'd said.

"And tell me again. Where did you find the postcard?"

She took the copy of 'Great Expectations' from her bag.

"In here."

"My, my, that looks like one of our editions, my dear. Quite an unusual set, probably worth a few bob, now. Not that I'd sell them of course. Too much sentimental value. Let's go and have a look at the bookcase."

How Chloe wished that Mrs Tiler could have been with her at that moment. She remembered the teacher talking about 'sentimental value'. There was some memory of a question about what three objects would you take from your house if there was a fire. Mrs Tiler said many people had chosen a family photograph. It wasn't worth much money but it was a reminder of love and happiness.

Chloe knew she must stop feeling sorry for herself. This was a great adventure, a real case for a detective. Then she realised there were no family photographs in their flat.

"Are you all right my dear?" asked Mr Cooper. "Something worrying you? You're quite safe here you know."

And Chloe realised that was right, she did feel quite safe with Mr Cooper. This was no time or place for daydreaming.

They both walked down to the bookcase and Chloe watched as Mr Cooper examined the titles. "Let me see your copy again."

"Do you know, Chloe? I think that book belongs here. I haven't checked them for… I don't know how long… could be at least two years. But that's remarkable, isn't it? Who gave you the book?"

Chloe could not really explain why, even to herself, but for some reason she was reluctant to say it was her mother. "Someone gave it to me. I don't know them very well."

She was sure she was blushing but Mr Cooper just raised his eyebrows in a questioning way.

"A mystery, a case for Sherlock Holmes perhaps. But I know who we should ask. I'll talk to Kirsty. Come back at the same time next Monday. Just leave the postcard with me. It's been a pleasure to meet you, Chloe."

Chapter Twelve
Daisy

Chloe had not slept well the previous night, worrying about Mr Cooper and the postcard and the mention of 'Kirsty'. Perhaps it was her mum. Perhaps it wasn't. Her mind had twisted and knotted in crazy circles. It had to be her mum. Her name was Kirsty and she had given her, Chloe, the copy of 'Great Expectations'. And it was identical to the other Dickens' books in The Jubilee library. But no, surely not, it must be a coincidence. She couldn't quite tie her mum up with The Jubilee Hotel and Mr Cooper. They didn't seem to fit somehow.

She had been woken from her fretful dreams by her mum knocking on her bedroom door, telling her it was half past eight and she was off to work.

"You'll need to get up, my girl," her mum had said crossly. "And you'll need to sort out that hound of yours."

"All right, Mum, sorry Mum…"

Mum had vanished.

Chloe had just finished pulling on her sweater, when there was a loud knocking at the door. Who could that be? She wasn't used to visitors. Her mother never encouraged them.

She went to the closed door and shouted.

"Who is it?"

"It's me."

"Who's 'me'?"

"Me of course, who d'you think it is?"

By this time, Chloe had recognised the voice. Her heart sank;

she was in no mood for Daisy. And what was she doing here anyway? She shouldn't be wandering about the streets. She should be at home with her mum. And Daisy was so bossy. She liked to take control of Chloe, but Chloe had a dog to look after and a plan to make. What should she do about her mum? Ask her a direct question? Was she the 'Kirsty' Mr Cooper talked about?

She opened the door and Daisy sauntered in as if she was the landlord doing an inspection.

"Bit small, isn't it?"

"It suits us," said Chloe. "Easy to maintain." Recalling something her mum had once said. "And Daisy, don't take your jacket off, we're going to take Laika for her morning walk and loo stop. Here's the bag and scoop, that can be your job."

Daisy pulled a pained face but, for once, did as she was told and followed Chloe down the stairs. But she couldn't resist saying how dirty they were.

Chloe ignored the remark and ran with Laika to the park.

"Do your job then, Daisy. Get on with it. Can't leave it there for someone to walk on. You can be fined, you know, for not clearing it up; it can be very nasty for small children. It gives them some nasty disease."

"All right Choe, all right, don't go on about it. I do know what to do. My granny's got a pedigree something or other."

"She would have," said Chloe sharply.

And so they returned to the flat. The day had not started very well for either girl.

Daisy was not impressed by Laika. "That is one 'orrible dog."

"No, she isn't, she's beautiful."

Chloe was not amused.

"Her name is Laika and you will be nice to her – otherwise

I shall ask you to leave."

"I might refuse."

Daisy was used to getting her own way.

"And I might insist."

Chloe had grown bolder since she and Daisy had last crossed swords.

"And Daisy, what are you doing here anyway? How did you know where I lived?"

And just like her mum had done on Saturday, to Chloe's considerable surprise, Daisy slumped onto the sofa, buried her head in her lap and started sobbing. Chloe responded by sitting next to her, putting her arm round her shoulders, gently and uncertainly at first, and then more confidently, as Daisy's sobs turned to hiccupping with occasional tears streaking down her cheeks.

Finally, Daisy tried to explain. "My mum's been going out sometimes, leaving me alone for a bit and telling me to do the work that Mrs Tiler sends on the computer. But, some of it's really hard – like that stupid multiplication of fractions – and I can't do them and then when Mum comes back, she's cross with me 'cos I haven't done any work."

She paused for breath and blew her nose with a mangled-looking tissue before carrying on.

"And I hate being on my own. I always think that corona whatsit is going to slide under the door and get me. And it's not like a monster or a ghost, is it Chloe? You can see them, but you can't see…" and she paused for some time before exploding… IT!"

She stopped to blow her nose with the tissue that was now in tatters.

"And then Mrs Tiler sent me an email explaining how to do

them fractions – but I still can't do them. They're just stupid. When I'm a model, I bet I won't have to do stupid old multiplication of fractions – or use a semicolon."

Chloe smiled to herself but tried to look sympathetic. She understood exactly how Daisy felt about being on her own a lot, as well as her fear of the invisible virus. She felt pleased that Daisy had come to confide in her. That for once, Daisy was leaning on her rather than acting all superior. Maybe, in time, she'd be able to tell her secrets to Daisy. It would be so good to have a friend of her own age to talk to.

Daisy looked up and peered tearfully round the room.

"Do you have a computer, Chloe?"

"No, we don't."

"Ipad?"

"No. Mum says we can't afford those things."

"You're lucky then."

"Why's that?"

"Because that silly school can't bother you."

"My mum does have a mobile, though, and she does get texts sometimes. Perhaps Mrs Tiler will contact her."

"Maybe later, it's the Easter Holidays soon."

Chloe felt for the first time that she and Daisy might be able to talk honestly.

"How did you know where I lived, Daisy?"

"Well, you remember that time you came to tea and we went to my bedroom. I have that 'Friends Forever' book and I got you to fill in one of the pages at the back. You know, name, birthday, favourite colour, all that stuff. And you had to put in your address and phone number."

"Oh, yes, I'd forgotten that. Didn't have a phone number."

"No, you didn't, otherwise I'd have phoned you."

Chloe decided not to tell Daisy about her new mobile phone. Well, it wasn't exactly new, probably about fifteenth hand, but at least it still worked. Best not tell Daisy at the moment though.

Chloe decided, though, that she must be straight with Daisy about how things were.

"You do know, Daisy, that we're supposed to stay in our own houses unless we're exercising?"

"How come you know so much about it all?"

"Because I like to know what's going on, even if it's pretty scary. So I watch the news on the telly in the morning when Mum's at work."

"My mum won't let me watch it. She says it's best not to know too much – and anyway, I was just exercising on the way here. I even passed a policewoman and she just grinned at me. That's all. I grinned back. End of story."

Chloe decided not to have an argument with Daisy about whether or not children of their age should know what was going on – but she didn't want her mum catching them together in the flat.

"My mum would go crazy if she found you here."

"Well, she won't, will she. Doesn't she go to work?"

"Most days, yes, but not the weekends. Daisy, it would be good to meet sometimes, but we'll have to be very careful."

"What's to stop us meeting up in the park – me doing my exercise and you walking that... thing... that dog."

"And," shrieked Daisy suddenly, "there's something to celebrate."

"What's that?" asked Chloe.

Daisy started to clap her hands above her head and dance round the room.

"No SATs, no SATs, no SATs, they can't make us do SATs

now. Hooray, hooray, hooray. Three cheers for no SATs…"

Daisy's dance moves grew more complicated. Chloe joined her though rather half-heartedly; she wasn't used to dancing.

"Three cheers for no SATs. Hip, hip… hooray, hip, hip, hip… hooray…"

This excitement was cut short by a phone playing a pop song very loudly, a woman's voice, probably American. Chloe had no idea who it was.

"Oh no," said Daisy peering at the screen, "it's my mum! She's wondering where I am."

"Just tell her you've been exercising. You can get back pretty quickly from here. Now go!"

Daisy paused and gave Chloe a little hug. "Friends?"

"Friends," said Chloe. "I'll see you at the park on Tuesday, ten o'clock. Wait ten minutes. If I don't turn up, go home. I'll do the same."

"Just like a spy film," said Daisy.

"Exactly," said Chloe.

After Daisy had gone, Chloe wondered whether she was quite as happy as Daisy was about there being no SATs. A bit of her had been looking forward to the challenge. Still, it was good to have Daisy as a friend – for the time being at least.

Chapter Thirteen
Follow That Mum!

The following day was Friday, last day of Mum's working week, and the last chance to try to find out where she actually worked. It just might be The Jubilee Hotel. Of course, she might go somewhere quite different to work. She might know Mr Cooper anyway, nothing to do with work. How complicated it all was!

She was up bright and early. Her mother noticed this straightaway.

"What are you up to my girl? You're usually still lounging in bed at this hour. Got a date, have you?"

Her mother winked and grinned at her. Chloe relaxed; her mum seemed to be in a good mood. She'd just play along with it.

"Sure have, mystery dog to prepare for Cruft's. Obedience class special."

Her mum laughed. That was good. Then her voice changed, serious stuff to follow.

"Forgot to tell you, Chloe. Had a text from the school yesterday. They're concerned about the fact we haven't got a computer or anything – blooming cheek if you ask me – and they don't want you to 'get behind'. That helper woman, Ma Baker, is dropping something round after one o'clock today. You must be here at that time – without fail! Got it?"

"Yes Mum, I've got it. Have a nice day."

Chloe had been thinking of the best way to follow her mum, and she'd been finding it difficult. She'd occasionally seen a film on the telly when some policeman or spy or some such person was trying to follow somebody suspicious. Often, of course, they were in cars and she remembered a film where a man with a briefcase and a moustache in a foggy London, had leapt into the road, stopped a taxi and shouted, 'Follow that white Jag. And don't lose it!'

But this was quite different. No car, no false moustache, no mistakes please. Please God, help me today, even if I can't find out where mum works.

Mum went, banged the door, leaving just silence and a very jittery Chloe, who counted to twenty and slid down the stairs clinging to the bannisters as she went. At the bottom, she panicked. She had meant to take the 'doctor's letter' in case she was stopped. How stupid. She raced back up the stairs, found the letter hidden under her mattress on the bed, and rushed down again.

She opened the main door cautiously – not that there was much point in being careful at this point. Her mother would be well on her way by now, wherever it was she was headed. She peered in the direction she thought her mum would take if she was going to The Jubilee. No sign of her at all. Nothing. Nobody. An empty pavement, just an old newspaper blowing across the street.

Then she had an idea. Why not run as fast as she could and hide in the doorway of that Chinese grocer's at the other end of Edmund Street? The shop had black blinds up at all the windows. It must have shut down like most of the others. Surely, if her mother was going to the hotel, she would approach it from the other end of the street, just as she had the other day. Chloe would have to pelt down Hammond Drive to the sea front, turn left into Jubilee Parade and reach the opposite end of Edmund Street that way.

Chloe ran as fast as she could along Hammond Drive, stopping only to tie a shoelace. Just after she started running again, she realised that three young men – probably only boys, although she couldn't see them very clearly because of the hoods and the black masks they seemed to be wearing – were headed for her at some speed on the same side of the road as she was. One of them was riding with the front wheel high in the air, thrust threateningly towards her at head height. She quickly crossed the road to avoid them. To her horror, they slowed down, crossed the road and came at her again, only this time much more slowly and with greater menace. She froze with fear, unable to move. She prayed to God that they would just pass by without harming her. They rode round her once in a circle, cat-calling and laughing at her, pretending they had bad coughs and calling her Covid-face and virus Vera.

She was saved by an elderly woman coming out of a house with a cracked windowpane, struggling with a walking stick and a shopping trolley. She bravely stepped into the circle, waved her stick in their faces.

"You mind our bikes, old lady, we'll sue you if you do any damage."

She fought back immediately. "Don't be so ridiculous. You mind your manners – and stop picking on old ladies and young girls. Is that the best you can do? Pathetic! I'll call the police if you don't scarper at once. Now go!"

They did. Chloe watched the bikes disappear quickly towards Seaview and breathed a sigh of relief.

"Oh, thank you, thank you." She clung to the old lady's arm for a moment. "You saved my life."

"I doubt that dearie, but I've never been one to put up with that sort of nonsense. Three of them against one little girl, cowards and bullies the lot of them. If my Jimmy were still alive, he'd have walloped them, good and proper. Now you take care. You shouldn't be out on your own you know. Where's your mum?"

A good question. Chloe wished she knew the answer.

She lied. "I'm just delivering a note from her to the doctor. I'll be back home again soon. Thanks again."

Chloe was badly shaken by the episode with the boys on the bikes. It made her realise she wasn't invisible, that she was pretty vulnerable walking about the streets on her own. She took a deep breath and thanked God for the old lady and for keeping her safe. She liked the way the old woman had said that Jimmy would have 'walloped' them. Jimmy must have been her husband, presumably dead by now, but he was still important to his wife and she was still proud of him. 'Walloped' was a great word. She would like to have seen Jimmy in his younger days, giving those boys a good thrashing. But now, she must be brave and carry on.

She reached Jubilee Parade and its breath-taking view of the sea, which was quite calm with no boats in sight. Chloe stopped for a moment and stared. She loved looking at the sea in all its moods and realised she had not been down this far since the lockdown had started. Still, no time to lose, her mother could walk quite fast when she was in the mood and Chloe knew she must get to her hiding place.

Just as she turned the corner into Edmund Street, Chloe got the shock of her life. Someone was huddled in there already. And that someone was her mum. And that someone was smoking a cigarette.

Chloe stopped at once, turned round and ran across the road towards the beach without stopping for a large, white van which hooted at her angrily. She jumped down onto the pebbles, sat against the wall, tears filling her eyes. Why, oh why, was everything going wrong again? Her first thought was how angry she was at her mum for smoking again. She thought she'd given up the horrible habit. But obviously she hadn't. Chloe tried to breathe more slowly and think about what to do next.

It wasn't certain that her mum was heading for The Jubilee Hotel but it was pretty likely. She was very close to it; the coincidences were growing and growing. Sherlock Holmes would have gone through the evidence. First: the copy of 'Great Expectations' her mother had given her; secondly: Mr Cooper saying that her copy was definitely from the hotel; thirdly: Mr Cooper saying that Kirsty might know something and Kirsty was her mother's name; fourthly: arranging to meet her at the hotel on Monday, knowing that he would be seeing Kirsty on Friday; and sixthly (stupid word), her mum was having a nasty fag in a doorway not far from the hotel.

At least she wasn't smoking at home at the moment. Chloe had heard that it was very hard to give up cigarettes; she supposed her mum was making an effort by only smoking out of the flat. But there was no way she could say anything to her about it! There was no way she could hang about outside the hotel now; she would have to go home, wait for Mrs Baker and see what the schoolwork was like. She wasn't particularly keen on the multiplication of fractions, but she knew she found them easier than Daisy did. They would keep her busy for a bit. Daisy's outburst had made her think. On her sad trudge back home, Chloe was trying to think of a job in the future where the multiplication of fractions might come in useful, but apart from being a maths teacher, she couldn't think of any.

Mrs Baker was very punctual. On the stroke of one o'clock there was a knock on the door. Chloe waited a moment, and following her mother's instructions, opened it slowly. You never knew who it might be. Although this time it was the person she was expecting, Mrs Baker clasping a big brown envelope and smiling in a slightly forced manner whilst peering nosily at the flat.

"Well, here you are Miss Hopper, one pile of work. See if you can finish it by the time the next term starts. I don't think we'll be back in school by then but there's plenty can be done at home." She hardly paused for breath. "Your mum in? You shouldn't be on your own."

Just gone to the shop," said Chloe. "You might meet her on the stairs."

Mrs Baker took the hint to leave, although of course, there was no chance of passing Mrs Hopper on the stairs.

Chloe closed the door behind her and opened the envelope. Exactly right. Multiplication of fractions – amongst other things.

Chapter Fourteen
More Questions Than Answers

For a long time, Chloe had felt it would be good if she could play the part of a tough police inspector interrogating her mum. There would be a huge but silent constable in the corner, with her mum sitting nervously behind a table, pretending to the inspector that she didn't smoke. There would be one dim light overhead and the inspector would turn on the recording. "Inspector Michael Watson and Police Constable James Martin with Mrs Kirsty Hopper. Fifteen hundred hours Saturday April 25th 2020."

"Mrs Hopper – or may I call you Kirsty?"

"Kirsty's fine with me. Don't like to remember Mr Hopper."

"Why haven't you asked for a solicitor?"

"Don't need one. Nothing to hide."

"Why don't you like to remember Mr Hopper?"

"He's best forgotten, that's all. Better off without him."

"But you've kept his name. Why is that?"

Kirsty paused.

"I will have that cigarette if you don't mind."

"No problem at all Kirsty, no problem at all."

The huge, silent constable produced an ashtray. Kirsty lit up and took a huge lungful of smoke. She coughed.

"So, why have you kept his name?"

"Because it's better with a child, that's why. What's that word? Respectability. Better to be Mrs than Miss or Ms. I have enough problems with some of those women at school I can tell you. Better for Chloe."

"Who's Chloe?"

"She's my lovely daughter."

"How old is she?"

"Eleven."

"Does she want to know about Mr Hopper?"

"Yes, she does."

"Do you answer her questions?"

"No, I don't."

"Why is that Kirsty?"

"Because she's better off not knowing."

"When she's eighteen she'll have a right to know the answers."

"But she's not eighteen now, is she?"

"Were you and Mr Hopper married?"

"We were."

"Is he still alive?"

Long pause. Kirsty lights another cigarette.

"I believe so."

"When did you last see him?"

"About nine years ago?"

"Do you know where he is?"

"No idea."

"Are you divorced?"

"Do I have to answer that question?"

"No, I suppose you don't."

"Good, so I shan't tell you."

"You recently seem to have some sort of change in your life. Just a little more time to spend with Chloe, a little more money to spend, a bit less smoking and drinking. Is that right?"

Chloe's imagination often took flight but it provided no answers to those questions she so desperately wanted answered.

The inspector was no better than she was. But anyway, she was playing both parts. She tried to remember if her mum had ever said that she and her dad were married. Was she, Chloe, just making that up? Because it was nice to think that her parents had been married in some pretty country church with bridesmaids and red roses and champagne and... But then, deep down, she knew this was only a fantasy. If they had married, they certainly hadn't lived happily ever after!

And then there was the name itself, Hopper. Was his name really Hopper? Certainly, that was what her mum called herself and Chloe, but that didn't prove anything. She had frequently tried to get the answers but her mum wouldn't budge. She would give nothing away. She certainly wasn't going to ask her if she'd started smoking again.

But that last question of the Inspector's. That was a new one, the sudden increase in spending power – Saturday evening takeaways, gifts from Smiths, mobile phone for Chloe. She even thought her mum was wearing a new skirt and blouse. She looked really nice in them. Surely, they were new?

The time to ask a new question, softly, gently without any warning, would be Saturday evening after the takeaway. The bottle of red wine could well put her mum in a good mood.

She remembered a story Mrs Tiler had read them about children being evacuated during the war. It was the small episode about the farmer's wife who was looking after the children from London that Chloe remembered, because it was something she'd never thought about before.

It was to do with someone's 'maiden name'. She remembered Mrs Tiler saying that at that time, all the women who got married would have taken their husband's surname and become a 'Mrs'. She explained that before she met her husband, she had been Miss Barnes but because she married Mr Tiler, she became Mrs Tiler. So 'Barnes' was her maiden name. She did go on to explain that today many couples decided not to marry and, if they did, some would not take their husband's name and preferred to be a 'Miss' or a 'Ms' – or just be called by their first and second names without any title.

In the story the farmer's wife was called Mrs Gould, but she explained to the evacuees that her maiden name had also been Gould. So she had been Miss Gould and was now Mrs Gould. A cheeky boy in the story had asked her which Gould was it she had now? Single or double? Chloe thought that was quite funny although she wasn't really sure why.

Anyway, after much thought, she decided she'd ask her mother, softly, gently without any warning: "What was your maiden name Mum?"

Her mum had been going on about one of the female judges in the talent show they'd been watching – not really nasty or unpleasant, just rather critical. She didn't like her make-up or hairstyle. She also thought the name she used was obviously not her real name and made her sound silly. The use of the word 'name' was the trigger for Chloe's question.

"What was your maiden name, Mum?"

Her mum opened her mouth quite naturally as if to give Chloe a straight answer to a straight question. Then she closed her mouth and stared hard at Chloe. She grabbed the television remote and turned the volume right down. Both she and Chloe kept their eyes half on the silent screen and half on each other during their conversation. Her mum was the first to speak.

"That's a funny question, my girl. What brought that about?"

"Well, it suddenly struck me that I don't know it."

"When did it strike you?"

"Some of the work I got from Mrs Baker was an English practice test about the ways in which people make up their passwords for computer security, and how the companies check that you're the real person taking the money, or whatever. One of the things they can ask you is, 'What was your mother's maiden name?' So, I thought to myself, I don't know."

Her mother had obviously been thinking hard.

"I can't tell you, my love. One day, quite soon, I promise. I know you're growing up and you want to know about your dad and everything, but sometimes you have to be patient."

"But it's my life, Mum, I have a right to know."

"You do, eventually, but you're still a child."

She took Chloe's hands in her own and stroked them. It made Chloe realise that her mother never wore a ring.

"But Mum, what was your name at school? You must have had a name! Kirsty Somethingorother. Was it Hopper? Go on," Chloe pleaded, "please tell me, Mum. Was it Hopper? Or was it something else?"

Mum released her hands and looked at Laika lying snoozing in the corner.

"One day, Chloe, one day very soon, I will tell you all I can. But you'll have to wait a bit longer, you'll have to be very grown up, and you'll have to be very patient – and understanding. There may be things I'll find hard to explain. And that's that. Now, let's watch that quiz show and see if that bloke's going to take the two hundred and fifty thousand or risk another question."

"One last question tonight, Mum. Please, please pretty please."

"Well, I suppose I can always refuse to answer."

"Last Saturday, when you were very upset, did you also hear something about getting some extra money from somewhere?"

Her mother stood up, went over to Laika and stroked her – probably the first time she'd done so.

"Perhaps, Chloe, perhaps. Now, sit down, watch the telly and leave the questions to the millionaire man."

And Chloe had to settle for that – for the time being at least. There was the appointment with Mr Cooper to come on Monday. Who knew what that might reveal?

Chapter Fifteen
Monday Morning Surprises

There was an interesting start to the day; Mum appeared in the sitting room wearing a dark blue suit Chloe had never seen before. Her lipstick looked a brighter shade of red and the eyeliner a deeper black. But certainly, very smart – fit enough for Buckingham Palace.

"Gosh, Mum, are you going to a wedding or an interview?"

Her mum grinned.

"Gosh, Chloe, you're getting a bit too sharp for your own good. You might cut yourself if you're not careful. How about 'Gosh, Mama, you're looking quite stunning today'?"

Chloe couldn't imagine this version of her mother sneaking a fag in the shop doorway. The appearance of this smart new lady might mean that she wasn't going to The Jubilee Hotel and that, perhaps, just perhaps, Mr Cooper knew that – and that was why he'd asked Chloe to come today.

"Well, you certainly are. Am I allowed to ask if you're going to work as usual today?"

"You may ask, and no, I'm not."

"Am I allowed to ask where exactly you are going?"

"You may ask, and no, I'm not going to tell you."

This time Chloe grinned.

Chloe was beginning to feel that she and her mum, were beginning to have a rather more grown up relationship. She wasn't so worried that her mum would react so sharply to every question she asked. Perhaps it had something to do with the

Lockdown. Perhaps it had something to do with the 'Saturday Morning Letter'.

Her mum suddenly screamed. Without any warning, Laika had moved towards her and was about to jump up, with dirty paws scrabbling at her fresh blue skirt.

Chloe moved quickly and grabbed Laika, pulling her away.

Just for a moment Mum was shaken out of her confident stride.

"Lucky for you, my little dog, that you didn't get me. That could have been the end of you."

Chloe knew her mother was probably only half-joking. She was beginning to come round to the dog and, as one of the two people who put food in her bowl, Laika was certainly out to charm her. But that was a near miss. Chloe couldn't bear to think of the consequences.

"Time you were going Mum. Before that dog does any real damage."

"I think you're right my girl. Have a good day."

"Love you, Mum."

"Love you, daughter."

"And by the way, Chloe. I don't like you being left on your own. It's not right. From tomorrow, I'm taking a couple of weeks off."

And with that the lady in the blue suit was gone.

Chloe's attention was grabbed by Laika who was in great need of her morning walk; she was already looking much healthier and had started bringing her lead to Chloe to show her exactly what was expected. Chloe would need to tire her as much as she could, so that Laika would be ready for a sleep while she was out visiting Mr Cooper at the hotel.

With nobody else in sight on this grey Monday morning, it

was fairly cold with a faint covering of frost on the grass. Chloe was glad to run as fast as she could to keep up with Laika, pulling strongly on her lead. Chloe was not ready to risk her running free. Who knows what terrible things might happen to her? She loved this scruffy dog so much; the thought of any harm coming to her gave Chloe a shiver of fear in her stomach.

Chloe was lost in her thoughts about the day ahead. Would any secrets be revealed? What, if any, was the link between Mr Cooper and her mum? Would Daisy turn up at the park the following morning.

"Excuse me miss, do you think you could stand still for a moment, please?"

Chloe skidded to a halt, holding Laika with some difficulty, before becoming aware of a large policeman, breathing quite heavily, coming up behind her. They had stopped by a park bench.

"We'll sit down if you please," said the policeman, still catching his breath.

"I'm Police Constable Wayne Davidson and I need to ask you a few questions."

"May I join you?" came another squeakier voice.

Chloe was suddenly overcome by the sudden turn of events. She sat down nervously on the bench and looked up to see who it was who wanted to join the party. She was terrified she might be in trouble with the policeman for being out alone or something. But what she saw turned her fear into astonishment.

Standing in front of the bench was a large ape, gorilla or orang-utan or some such creature. He/she/it spoke again.

"Is it all right if I sit down as well? My name's Darren, I don't mean any harm. In fact, you could say I mean a lot of good."

The policeman was obviously equally astonished and was starting to bring out his radio or phone or whatever it was.

"Now look here, Darren. The first thing is that, because of social distancing…"

He was interrupted by a loud bark from Laika who really wasn't at all sure about what kind of creature Darren was. She jumped on to Chloe's lap for protection.

"As I was saying, because of social distancing regulations, I cannot allow you to join us on the bench. I am sitting at one end of it and the young lady at the other. If you were to sit in the middle it would contravene the present government regulations. And we can't have that, can we?"

"Oh, certainly not, officer, certainly not. I am not one to contra… anything. I'll stand over here at something like the required two metres."

Chloe thought about asking to be excused but this was turning into something totally unexpected, and possibly, amusing. But she'd have to be careful; she was planning carefully what she was going to tell the policeman. She felt in her pocket – she still had the envelope with 'Doctor Keith' written on it. Something to tell Daisy, anyway – unless she were in prison, of course.

The policeman took out a black notebook and, just like the policeman Chloe had once seen at a pantomime, a stubby pencil which he proceeded to lick. We'll start with you Darren, I think.

"Name and address please."

"Darren Ape, 55 Cage Drive, Seabourne Zoo."

The policeman had started to write that down, and then stopped.

"Now, look here Darren, or whatever your name is, this is not a moment for humour. We are living in an unprecedented time of pandemic and Lockdown. You realise I could arrest you and have you locked up."

Darren looked thoughtful, well as thoughtful as was possible for a man dressed up as a gorilla.

"That could be excellent publicity if you did arrest me, officer. What would I have to do to be arrested? I can imagine the headline now. Seabourne Gazette front page – PC Snapper locks up gorilla raising money for the NHS crisis."

The policeman gave a big sigh. He realised he was being made fun of, and he didn't like it, but he had to get out of the hole he'd dug for himself.

"Oh, I get you, Darren. You're in fancy dress and you're raising money for the NHS coronavirus appeal for much needed equipment for frontline staff?"

"Got it in one officer. Well done. I just patrol the streets and ask everybody to put something in the bag – cash only. As you know, officer, people want to get rid of their cash at the moment, what with everything being paid for by credit cards. So, I'm doing very well."

And from his large gorilla pocket Darren produced a very large bag.

"Perhaps you'd like to make a donation, officer?"

Once again, the policeman was unsure as to the best action to take.

"Actually, Darren, I never carry money with me. Too risky in my line of work."

"Well, in that case, I won't bother you any further. I wish you, and this delightful young lady and her delightful dog, a very good morning."

The policeman wasn't going to let him go so easily.

"And you never know, officer, it might not be a real dog. It might be an accomplice of mine raising money for the NHS."

The policeman could not allow Darren to escape so easily.

"Do you have any means of identification or a licence or anything?"

Darren just turned and raced across the park at great speed, disappearing into the grey Monday morning distance. The policeman breathed very deeply again. Chloe knew he had no chance at all of catching Darren. She was also wondering whether Darren was a con-man, or someone really raising money for the NHS. She hoped it was for the NHS – that would be a great thing to do, as well as being rather funny. Perhaps she'd come across him again.

The policeman obviously felt he had to retrieve some of his dignity with the girl sitting at the other end of the bench.

"And now, young lady, what exactly is it you're up to?"

For a moment, Chloe considered a number of cheeky answers. For some reason the lockdown, and the strange events connected with it, had given Chloe a confidence she had not felt before: 'I'm revising for a maths test. I'm training this dog to be a silent killer, I'm boiling an egg.'

But she knew that such replies would only annoy the policeman even more.

"I'm taking my dog, Laika, for her morning walk and having my exercise at the same time." She paused. "Is that Okay?"

The policeman thought about that for a moment.

"Better check your identity."

Chloe had not expected this, but she remained calm.

"I didn't know I had to have something to prove who I am. But you can check that the dog's for real and my mum's phone number is on the disc."

As soon as she'd said that, she had this horrible image of her mum being interviewed by old men in dark suits, sitting on an upright chair in a large room with faded paintings of riders in red on the wall. Her phone would make that terrible noise of dogs barking. She'd forgotten to switch it off. She'd become flustered and rush out of the room leaving her bag behind on the floor.

"I don't think that will be necessary; I'll just take a note of it in case there are any further incidents."

Chloe tried to imagine what sort of 'incident' she'd been involved in. But, once again, decided to leave the policeman to bother other innocent people while she took Laika home.

Chapter Sixteen
Not The Best Afternoon

"Now then, Laika, you must be a very good girl while I'm out. You've had your food, there's plenty of water in your bowl, I'm sorry you didn't get as much exercise as you should have, but that was the policeman's fault…"

Laika gave a little bark and climbed onto the sofa. She seemed to know what was going on and was happy to snooze while her mistress was gone. Chloe checked her possessions: phone, key, doctor's letter, purse containing about £2.65. How her life had changed since this coronavirus thingy had started! No school, a pet of her own, a mobile phone, a mystery to solve, a mother who'd changed quite a lot… She patted Laika's nose and was quickly on her way to The Jubilee Hotel.

She broke into a little trot because she didn't want to be late. Mr Cooper seemed nice enough but she'd only just met him. She didn't want to upset him. He obviously knew something – it was just a question of finding out what.

"Chloe! Chloe! Just stop for a moment, please! I can't keep up with you."

Chloe stopped to find Daisy standing beside her with her dark green school bag on her back. It looked as if it was very heavy.

"You're not very fit are you Daisy? You should get a dog."

"Oh, don't be like that, Chloe. I need you. I've got a favour to ask."

Chloe was suddenly grateful that she seemed to be gaining a

friend who needed her. And had a favour to ask. She softened and smiled.

"And what would that be?"

"It's all this school stuff we've got to do. It's too hard for me. You're the brainy one. I thought you could help me."

"I'm sorry, Daisy, I can't at the moment."

Chloe was thinking fast. There was no way she could tell Daisy what she was really up to.

"I'm… I'm on an errand for my mum."

"I'll come with you then."

Chloe's mind was racing.

"Does your mum know what you're up to?"

Daisy looked hard at Chloe.

"Does your mum know what you're really up to?" She paused. "My mum will be back by one. I'll be home by then. She'll never know I've been gone."

"Look Daisy, the best thing for us to do is to wait 'til tomorrow and do your work together then. We had planned to meet, remember? You can come to the flat instead of meeting in the park."

And then she remembered that her mum would not be working.

"Must warn you, Daisy. My mum will probably be there."

"That's Okay. By the way, can you do semicolons?"

"Probably."

"Thanks Chloe. High fives?"

They did and Daisy turned and staggered off in the opposite direction with her heavy bag. Chloe was intrigued to know just what Daisy had in her bag and thought about shouting after her, but decided against it. She was on a mission.

Not far from the hotel, just past the fish and chip shop with bars on the window and a metal grille on the door, Chloe saw two familiar figures who appeared to be sharing a cigarette. She was keen to pass by unnoticed so she crossed the road and stared down at the pavement rather than the two unusual characters talking animatedly on the other side of the street. No such luck.

"Ahoy there!" It was the gorilla. "Spare a dime for the NHS, young miss?" Darren paused and took a closer look. "Don't I know you?"

Chloe was determined to stay on her side of the road. As she shouted, "Don't know," a mud-spattered vehicle passed swiftly by, loud rap music blaring forth. It had probably once been a white van but was now as much black and grey as white. No sooner had it passed than Chloe realised she'd been joined by Darren, the gorilla, and the beggar with the posh voice she'd met the other day. He didn't seem quite as subdued as he'd been the other day.

"So, what are you up to young lady." His speech was rather slurred. "Read any more pages of Great Expectations? Met Miss Havisham yet?"

Chloe was desperate to get away.

"I'm sorry but I'm late."

And she raced off, turned the corner into Edmund Street and straight to the door of the hotel.

On previous occasions the door had been open but now it was securely locked with a huge notice: 'CLOSED UNTIL FURTHER NOTICE' on the door. There was a bell in the wall next to the door.

Chloe's mind was racing. Oh, what shall I do? Only one thing you can do my girl and that's ring the bell. She rang the bell. Or rather, she pressed the button in the wall but she couldn't hear anything. She had no idea whether or not the bell had worked. She pressed it again and waited. Nothing happened.

The hotel was semi-detached, with a bed and breakfast to the left and a scratched door in the wall on the right of the hotel. She tried the door. Locked – and probably bolted. She tried to push against it. No luck.

Perhaps there might be someone in the bed and breakfast house. They might know Mr Cooper, they might know something. Chloe was certainly growing braver so she walked up the steps and peered through the pane of glass in the door, which had an old-fashioned knocker. She couldn't locate a bell. So she banged the brass knocker against the wooden frame as hard as she could, feeling more and more frustrated. Nothing happened. Nobody came. She even lifted the letter box and shouted. She returned to the hotel and tried the letter box there – same result.

She suddenly felt downcast and quite sad. She had been sure Mr Cooper would be there and would start to unravel the mystery. But now, there was nothing she could do. Or was there? She remembered she had her mobile and that she had once phoned the number for Mr Cooper from the inside of the hotel by the reception desk. The number should be on her phone – after all she hadn't made many calls. She found what she was sure was the right number and pressed the phone to her ear. It rang and it rang and it rang and it rang. Not even a message. Time to go home.

She was anxious to avoid the gorilla and the beggar, so she approached the corner of the street cautiously, hoping they wouldn't see her. No sight of them. Great. At least one piece of luck on this difficult morning.

She couldn't wait to get home, to close the door behind her and give Laika a good cuddle. She raced up the stairs and opened the door which led straight into the sitting room. She wondered if the dog would still be asleep.

No, she wasn't asleep. In fact, she wasn't there at all. Laika had gone.

Chapter Seventeen
Topsy Turvy World

Chloe's first reaction was that there was a mistake. It was impossible for Laika to be missing. Despite the fact that the doors to the bedrooms were closed, she must be in the flat somewhere. She just had to be. Nothing else was possible. The only two people with keys to the flat were herself and her mum.

She opened the doors to the bedroom, looked under the beds, even called out her name. She pushed the beading aside to go into the galley but there was no room there for a dog to hide. She began to feel sick. She slumped onto the sofa and started to cry. She felt helpless, utterly helpless, she could think of no action she could take, other than wait for her mum's return – which was normally about half past two but who knows what time she would return today. Her dog, her beautiful, beautiful, little dog who was starting to know her and love her. Would she ever see her again?

Then a thought struck her. Where was her lead? It didn't take her long to realise that the lead was missing too. Somehow, someone had managed to get into the flat and kidnap the dog. But why? It wasn't as if Laika was one of those pedigree dogs Daisy had boasted about. As much as Chloe loved her, she couldn't imagine anyone giving money for her.

At that moment the door opened and her mother came in. Gone was the happy, confident woman who'd marched out of the flat in the morning. Taking off her coat, she came and gave her daughter a warm hug but Chloe thought her mum was trembling and might have been crying. Just like her – trembling and full of tears.

"Mum, Mum, I'm sorry, I'm sorry, I don't know how it could have happened but Laika has... Laika has gone m... missing."

She burst into tears again and her mum held her tightly before gently pushing her away and looking into her eyes.

"Let's sit down, Chloe, and we'll take this slowly."

They collapsed onto the lumpy sofa and Mum put her arm around Chloe's quivering shoulder. "Just tell me, Chloe, slowly."

"Well, I left Laika here while I went for a walk."

Her mother's eyes widened.

"But surely you take Laika with you when you go for a walk?"

"I do, normally, but I'd already taken her for a walk and when we got back, she seemed sleepy and I needed some more fresh air so I went back to the park."

Her mother looked deep into Chloe's eyes.

"There's something about this I don't like, Chloe. It seems wrong somehow. Are you lying to me?"

Chloe looked away, her face going red as she did so.

"Not now Mum, please, I'll explain everything but I must tell you about Laika."

"Well, I think you've told me. She's not here. I can see that. And I can see that you have no idea where she is."

Chloe fought back the salty tears.

"Do you, Mum, do you?"

"Well, I can't be certain, but I do have an idea. I'm just going to make a phone call."

Her mum stood up, straightened her smart blue skirt, now looking a bit crumpled, and pulled her mobile from a hidden pocket. She made the call standing up. There seemed an eternity of waiting until she spoke – in her confident 'don't mess with me' voice.

"Is that you, Mr Kitchener? It's Kirsty Hopper. (Pause)Would I be right in thinking that you have in your possession one little dog named Laika, probably now very frightened and bewildered, kidnapped from my flat? (Pause) That's fine, we'll expect you in about five minutes."

"You know who he is, don't you Chloe? He's our landlord and he came in here, without my permission, to have a poke around while he thought I was out. There are three keys to the flat, and being the landlord, he has the third. He probably waited 'til you'd gone and made his move as soon as you disappeared. Now, whether or not he'd realised there was a dog here, I don't know. But, as I told you, we're not supposed to have pets without permission and when he came in and saw the dog, he decided to give us a fright."

"But Mum, is he allowed to come in without permission?"

"No, he isn't, and whether he is or not, no one, I repeat no one, at this time of coronavirus is allowed to go into someone else's house except in a medical emergency…"

She was stopped in full flow by a firm knock on the door.

She opened the door to reveal a short, stocky man with a beard, holding Laika by her lead. She was pulling to get in.

"Just let her go, Mr Kitchener."

He did but also made a move to come in himself.

"Don't you dare come in, Mr Kitchener. I could have you arrested for this you know. There's a pandemic crisis – in case you didn't know. You should stay locked down in your own home and not go around kidnapping other people's dogs."

His voice was surprisingly high; for some reason Chloe thought that a man with a beard would have a deep voice.

"Don't you 'don't you dare' me, Mrs Hopper. No cause for

you to get on your high horse. This flat does not belong to you, so it is not 'your flat'. You signed an agreement which states quite clearly that no pets are allowed here. So I did not, as you so crudely put it, 'kidnap' the dog – I was within my rights to remove an animal which was trespassing on my premises."

"'Trespassing!' That's a ridiculous word to use. A dog can't 'trespass'. What are you going to do? Take Laika to court? You trespassed, coming in here without the tenant's permission, having made no attempt to arrange a convenient time. And, what's more…" she paused, stabbing her forefinger in Mr Kitchener's direction, her voice growing more shrill, with every word, "we have established there's a pandemic problem and you should not be entering the flat, spreading the virus and endangering our lives."

"That's an outrageous thing to say. I am not spreading the virus. I don't have any of the symptoms."

"How are we supposed to know that? Have you been tested?"

Mr Kitchener clearly felt that the conversation was getting out of hand. He changed his tone to something softer and more reasonable.

"Why don't you sit down, Mrs Hopper? I'll stay here in the doorway at least two metres from you and we'll see if we can sort this out – you know what I mean, amicably, all friendly-like."

"I don't know if I'm feeling 'all friendly-like', as you put it. My daughter was terrified out of her wits when she came in to find the dog missing."

Mr Kitchener still tried to maintain his reasonable tone.

"Well, perhaps you shouldn't have encouraged her to have a dog on the premises, and what's more, as far as the police would be concerned, you shouldn't have let her out on her own for a long period of time. And…" he paused for effect, "you should have been here when she got back."

There followed an uneasy silence. Chloe's mum chose to break it. She spoke slowly.

"Have you quite finished, Mr Kitchener?"

The landlord's tone softened a little.

"Not quite, Mrs Hopper. There was another matter I wanted to discuss with you."

"And what's that?"

"I assure you this is not to do with the dog being here, Mrs Hopper, and I can assure you too that it's nothing to do with you being a bad tenant. You've always paid the rent on time, and apart from the flat being in a bit of a mess with the beginnings of that 'doggy smell' that comes with our canine friends, I've no complaints."

Chloe could see that her mum was starting to realise where this was leading. She gripped Chloe's hand tightly in a reassuring way. Mr Kitchener continued.

"For various personal reasons, I've decided I'd like to repossess the flat and…" he could see that Chloe's mum was poised to strike, "I'm sure we could come to a financial agreement satisfactory to both parties."

There followed another uneasy silence.

"And what are the details of this financial agreement?"

"If you vacate in a month's time, I'll give you this coming month and another two months' rent free, gratis and for nothing."

Chloe could sense her mother's brain whirring. What was she going to say? If she did accept, where on earth would they live?

Chloe's mum stood up and looked Mr Kitchener in his bloodshot eye.

"I'll agree – but only if we can keep the dog here." Another pause. "Deal?"

Mr Kitchener smiled. "Deal!" And he stuck out his hand for Kirsty to shake.

She was having none of that.

"Don't be silly, Mr Kitchener. No one is shaking hands at the moment. But just to let you know, I'm very happy with the deal – details of which, by the way, I shall need in writing before the end of the day. I was about to give notice anyway. Chloe and I will be moving out as soon as we can arrange the transport to move our few bits and pieces." She paused while both Chloe and her landlord tried to take in what had just been said. "Have a nice day Mr Kitchener."

Chapter Eighteen
Smoke Gets in Your Eyes

"I know what you're going to say, Chloe, and I do know why you're finding everything so hard to understand."

"But Mum, please say something. Please! My life is being turned upside down but I've no idea at all why. You've just told that horrid, little man that we're moving out but you haven't said where we're going. That's just so annoying, really annoying. Are we moving from Seabourne? Are we going to another small flat with no bathroom? Have you just won the lottery?"

"The answer to all those questions is no."

And then her mum's tone changed, became more soothing, more sympathetic.

"Come and sit next to me and I'll try to tell you what is going to happen. And I'm going to make you a promise, Chloe. All being well, and as long as there are no more nasty surprises, by tomorrow evening you will know where you're going and you'll have a better understanding of who exactly you are. I would have told you today but something happened this morning which I'm going to have to sort out tomorrow morning."

"Does that mean you're going out again tomorrow? You said you'd be at home from now on."

"I know I did, but something's come up. I'm just hoping that tomorrow will make things clearer. But, and I'm making my promise again, by tomorrow evening you'll know everything – warts and all."

"What does that mean, Mum? Warts and all."

"Well, a wart is a nasty little thing, that can grow on your skin – not necessarily serious but it doesn't always look very nice. I suppose it means that in people's lives, bad things can happen as well as good things. There are things we can be proud of and things we wish hadn't happened. So, you'll hear the good and the bad."

"Does some of this concern my father?"

Her mum didn't speak for some time. Finally, she took Chloe's hands and stroked them. Mother and daughter were both weeping quietly.

"Yes, it does."

"Is he still alive?"

Big pause.

"Yes, he is."

"I mean, is he my real father? Am I adopted or something?"

"No you are not adopted, he is your real father."

"Tomorrow, am I really going to find out more about him?"

Pause.

"Yes, you are… or certainly by the day after tomorrow at the latest."

"Am I going to see him soon?"

Her mum dropped Chloe's hands and stood up, suddenly agitated.

"I've made my promise and I'll keep it, Chloe. But you are going to have to be one very brave girl." Then her mum smiled. "It won't be a perfect ending, Chloe. We won't live happily ever after like in a fairy story. But I promise you again, it should be better than it is now. I sometimes wish I hadn't been so secretive but then you'll see why I've kept some things from you when you know what they are. You're growing up now and that means facing up to things."

Chloe wasn't sure how she'd survive 'til the following day – or even the day after that. She was certain she'd sleep badly, probably even worse than Christmas Eve. Not that tomorrow would be anything like Christmas, but she already had that ache in her stomach, that came when she was nervous, excited, or frightened – only this time it was all of those emotions at once. Chloe decided she'd try to change the mood.

"I know, Mum, let's play a game. It's still only the afternoon and it's ages 'til tomorrow."

"Haven't you got any school work to do?"

"I've done it."

"Are you sure?"

"Certain sure."

"What about that Charles Dickens book I gave you?"

"It's really lovely Mum, but I couldn't concentrate on it now."

"Okay, so what do you want to play?"

"Hide and Seek."

"In this flat? Are you trying to be funny?"

"Yes. It was a silly joke. How about Scrabble? We got it for Christmas and we've hardly ever played. I play at school sometimes, so I know the rules."

"I bet you do, young lady. And you're much better at spelling than I am."

"No, I'm not, and anyway it's not just spelling, it's vocabulary as well. You need a large vocabulary to be good at Scrabble – that's what Mrs Tiler says."

"You're fond of your Mrs Tiler, aren't you Chloe?"

Chloe wasn't sure how to answer.

"I like her a lot because she's friendly but firm with the naughty kids, so we don't have our lessons spoilt…"

Suddenly there was a shrill, shrieking noise. Chloe covered her ears with her hands. Laika was whining and barking pathetically. Chloe's mum was all action.

"Right, up you get. That's the fire alarm! You take the dog and I'll bring my handbag and your coat. Everything else can go up in flames for all I care."

"Oh Mum, don't be like that. Let's hurry up."

"Don't worry, Chloe, it's almost certainly a practice."

It wasn't. As soon as they'd opened the door, they could smell the smoke. Already it was getting hard to see the staircase. Chloe didn't want to cough but she couldn't help it.

"Right, you hold the handrail tightly, look down at the stairs, take one step at a time."

"Mum, this smoke's horrid. Laika's really scared."

"Give her to me. I'll hold her tight. Don't fret. We'll be fine, nearly down now."

As they struggled through the front door with five or six other people pushing and shoving, the disaster happened. An elderly lady following Chloe's mum stumbled in her anxiety and pushed Kirsty in the back. She tripped and, in doing so, lost control of Laika. The panicked dog raced past Chloe straight into the road. Fortunately, there was no traffic at that moment as the approaching Fire Engine was blasting its sirens and cars were keeping out of the way.

Chloe screamed. She caught sight of Laika streaking towards the park, then she lost sight of her. She took a step into the road and felt the wind of a heavy lorry racing by, regardless of the fire engine. She felt a heavy hand grip her arm. It was her mum.

"Don't you dare, Chloe. Stay here. Laika will be all right, you'll see."

Chapter Nineteen
Aftermath

During the night that followed, Chloe kept waking from nightmares. She was going down a winding staircase in the dark, the steps being so narrow on the inside that she had to walk on the wider bits on the outside. But there was no handrail on that wall and the tiles were both hot and slippery with damp at the same time. She could not get a firm hold and felt she was always about to fall, to tumble headlong through the smoke, down this everlasting staircase, to the familiar, scratched door at the bottom. She reached the door. It was locked. The smoke was blinding her, smothering her, she could hear the sirens but could see nothing. She screamed and sat up in bed.

Her mum came in and hugged her.

"There, there, my love. It's only a dream. You're quite safe. It's all over, There's no danger now."

Her mum stroked her face gently and sang a lullaby Chloe dimly remembered from her early childhood.

"Golden Slumbers, Kiss your eyes,
Smiles await you when you rise,
Sleep pretty wantons, Do not cry
And I will sing a lullaby."

It soothed her. It calmed her. She was desperately tired and fell at once into a deep sleep. But it was not long before the nightmares returned. She was standing on the edge of the pavement. A huge black lorry with headlights blazing and horn blaring was bearing down on her. She was holding Laika as tightly as she could but the little dog was pulling too hard. Chloe was weak, tired beyond hope, she would have to let go. In her dream she closed her eyes. She waited for the collision – one small, helpless dog, and one giant, black mass of thundering metal, that was the lorry. She screamed.

Her mum came into her room again.

"This time, my love, you're coming with me."

If Chloe had been awake enough, she would have been amazed at her mum's strength. She picked her daughter up and carried her gently to her own bed, before putting her down and cuddling up beside her.

"Now, just sleep, sleep. You won't be on your own. I shall be here."

And she kissed her daughter's forehead. And Chloe did sleep again, at once, and this time she fell into a deep space of nothingness, untroubled by nightmares.

The next time she crawled slowly into consciousness it was to be aware of her mum sitting on the edge of the bed with a mug of tea and a plate of ginger biscuits. Chloe sat up awkwardly; tea and biscuits in bed was a rare, almost unknown, treat. Her memory seemed foggy, clouded in distorted images and the sound of sirens and shouting. Then, as if a switch had been turned on, she was struck by the image of her standing on the side of the road with Laika pulling on the lead, the huge monster truck bearing down on the dog, racing headlong to what must have been a certain death.

Chloe took a sip of the tea and struggled to get out of bed. She must go and see if Laika was in the living room. She dared not ask her mum because she knew what the answer would be. Laika would not be there. But she had to see for herself. Her mum hugged her and smiled.

"There's a brave girl."

And suddenly there she was. Laika! Asleep in her box, quite still. For a horrible moment Chloe thought that it was a dead body but, no, surely her mum would not have allowed such a thing. Chloe now felt really unsteady on her feet and was sure she would faint if she did not lie down. She sank slowly to the floor and crawled towards Laika's box. She could see the dog was breathing, taking sudden uncertain breaths as if she too was reliving a nightmare. Chloe stroked her gently and spoke softly and reassuringly; it might have been wishful thinking but she was sure the breathing became less troubled and that there was a little wag of a sorry tail.

Chloe slumped onto the sofa as her mum came and sat close beside her, arm round the shoulder.

"Oh Mum, Mum, it's coming back to me… the fire… the smoke… the fire engine… the lorry… running into the park… you shouting and screaming…"

"It's all right, Chloe, it's all right. I know it seems like a nightmare now, but all is well. It wasn't as bad as your dreams, however horrific they were. Think of them as fears that actually never happened. And look at little Laika. She's fine, just fine."

"So, now Chloe," her mum's tone changed to her matter-of-fact voice, "I don't usually allow the television on in the morning, as you know, but I thought we might watch a bit of the local news – only if you're up to it, of course. It's not really very frightening and you might even see yourself! And it may put your mind at rest."

Chloe was startled and took her mother's arm away and looked at her closely.

"See myself? On the local news? Why?"

"Why do you think?"

"Because… because… because of the fire?"

"That's right. They told me it would be on about now."

The set was turned on and the familiar shape of the coronavirus occupied the screen – as usual. Then it faded. The presenter's voice was obviously changing tone.

"And now to other news. Yesterday evening, residents of 'The Outlook', a residential block of privately rented flats on Seaway at Seabourne, were evacuated when fire broke out on the ground and first floor flats."

(Pictures of the block of flats from the other side of the road, probably after the fire, with no sign of smoke. Then pictures of smoke pouring from first and ground floor windows.)

Fire engines were quickly on the scene and had the fire under control in about thirty minutes."

(Scenes of fire engines with hose pipes and firemen and police helping the residents, about thirty in all: scenes of people of various ages, at least one babe in arms and an elderly woman in a wheelchair.)

"Once the police had arrived, residents were escorted across the busy thoroughfare, to Nelson Park on the other side of the road. Residents from nearby houses came out with hot drinks in a show of typical Seabourne neighbourliness."

(Scenes in the park of neighbours with thermos flasks and plates of cake, offering blankets to the residents.)

"However, there were one or two scares. Eleven-year-old Chloe Hopper, who lives with her mother on the first floor, was traumatised when her pet dog, Laika, ran across the road out of her grasp."

(Pictures of the people pushing through the front door, glimpse of Kirsty on the ground, letting go of Laika, and the dog racing across the road into the park, followed by film of the large,

black truck racing by.)

"However, all was well a few minutes later when Chloe and her pet were reunited. Hazel Connors spoke to Chloe in the park."

(Film of interview with Hazel Connors and Chloe, who seems to be laughing and crying at the same time.

Hazel: Well, Chloe, you must be one relieved pet-owner.

Chloe: {after a long pause, somewhat bewildered} I am, yes I am.

Hazel: What were you thinking when your dog ran across the road?

Chloe: {finding her voice} Laika, she's called Laika.

Hazel: Okay then. What were you thinking when Laika ran across the road?

Chloe: I was thinking she'd be... she'd be... she'd be...

At this point, Chloe's mum stood up.

"I'm turning this off! This is dreadful! Bullying a child into an answer. I didn't know it would be like this... shocking!"

"No, Mum, don't turn it off! She was horrible, but I want to see it."

Hazel: Be what Chloe?

Chloe: {almost shouting} Killed! I thought she'd be killed.

Hazel: But she wasn't, was she?

Chloe: No, she wasn't.

Hazel: So how do you feel now?

{Long pause. Hazel moves the mike a little nearer to Chloe.}

Hazel: So how do you feel now?

Chloe: {Long pause} (tearfully) Good... good... well, better... *(starts to cry again)*

"So, all's well that ends well. One dog safe and well, one little girl, happily reunited with her pet. No one injured. Just one elderly smoker in a state of shock."

"Apparently, the fire had started in the room of one of the elderly residents who'd gone into the kitchen to make a cup of tea, forgetting he'd left an unfinished cigarette in the ashtray on the arm of his couch. The ashtray tipped over and the couch caught fire, creating a large amount of black smoke."

"An hour after the fire started, all the other residents were allowed to return to their homes. Apart from the elderly man, who has not been named. He was spending the night with relatives."

Mother and daughter were quiet for a moment. Mum stabbed the remote control angrily and the picture faded.

"That interview was a disgrace, Chloe, I shall have to make a complaint."

"Oh, don't Mum, please. It will only make it worse. I just want to forget it."

Mum looked hard at Chloe but said nothing.

Eventually Chloe spoke.

"Have you remembered Daisy's coming round this morning?"

"I have and I'm not happy, Chloe. It's not what people are supposed to be doing."

"What's that, Mum?"

"Going into other people's houses."

"And what about you, Mum? Are you doing what people are supposed to be doing?"

Her mother flinched.

"Don't spoil it, Chloe."

"Spoil what?"

"Our... our... relationship, my love. We have both worked hard lately and everything is about to change."

For a moment, Chloe doubted that the change was really about to happen. There had been so many false starts, half-promises that turned into thin air. But then, she had no choice. She had to trust her mum, to believe in what she'd said recently. That this very afternoon, Chloe's life would be transformed.

"Why has it all been so secret, Mum? I'm not a child you know."

"Well, you are a child still, in many ways. I do know that soon you will be a young woman and will have a right to know about your family's past. Once you know the truth, I do hope you will understand why I've had to tread carefully."

Chloe was excited but still angry with her mum.

"Okay, Mum, so I'm still a child, right." She paused. "I don't want to be left on my own with Daisy this morning."

There was a loud knock at the door.

"I think that bird has already flown Chloe. You'd better let her in. And… and… I promise I'll be back by twelve. And that will be that."

Chloe hugged her mum round the waist.

"Don't let me down Mum, please don't let me down."

She thought her mum was about to cry, but she stiffened and walked towards the door.

"I won't let you down, Chloe. I promise."

Daisy flew into the room.

"Hi, Mrs Hopper, hi Chloe, great to be out of the house for a bit."

And before Chloe even had the chance to say goodbye, her mum had vanished.

Chapter Twenty
Daisy, Daisy

Daisy dumped her huge school bag onto the floor and threw herself onto the sofa.

"That thing is so heavy."

Chloe picked it up to see just how heavy it was.

"You're right. Why did you bring everything? We're not going to need everything, Daisy."

"You're right enough there, Chloe. I only brought the lot because I can't be bothered to pack and unpack it and my mum told me I should bring it all. I've gotta tell you, Chloe, my mum is driving me up the wall. If this prison thing goes on much longer, I don't know what will happen. She'll end up hittin' me and I'll end up 'ittin' 'er."

She paused.

"Does your mum ever hit you, Chloe?"

"No, well maybe once or twice a long time ago when I was little. We've had some real arguments lately and she's looked at me as if she'd like to slap me, but she hasn't. The last couple of days, though, she's been... well, better in a funny sort of way. Hard to explain."

"What sort of better?"

"Sad, a bit, but mostly happier, as if we're going to have a better life all of a sudden."

Daisy stared at Chloe for a moment, shrugged and continued the attack on her mum.

"Yesterday, she looked at what I was doing – it was

alphabetical order – you know that dictionary stuff where you put the words in order – banana before biscuit and biscuit before butter and butter before buzz and so on – and she sat down and wrote a list of lots of words starting with 's' and 't' and told me to sort them. Some of them were really hard, like 'them' and 'their' and 'themselves'. So, I spent forever trying to do them while she was staring at that phone of hers and glaring at me from time to time. I got up once to go to the loo but she said I couldn't go 'til I'd finished the list. Just like that bossy Mrs Baker! Just like being back at school. And d'you know what happened after I'd finished them?"

She looked at Chloe.

"D'you know Chloe? Come on, what d'you think?"

"Sorry Daisy, I don't know."

"Guess."

"Oh, all right – she looked at them, marked them and you got them all right."

"No, she just grabbed them from me, tore the paper up, dumped it in recycling and said I could go to the loo. Didn't even look at them. I went to the loo after that and I was crying, I can tell you."

Chloe gave her a hug.

"I'm so sorry, Daisy. Being in lockdown with one other person is hard, isn't it?"

"It's all right for you, you've got a dog to take to the park – and you had that fire yesterday – must have been exciting. That fire. Saw the local news. Saw you on there talking to that Hazel woman. You was upset, weren't you?"

"I was, Daisy, very upset. My mum thinks that Hazel woman was bullying me to get a good story."

"That's what my mum said – 'it made for good telly'."

"Well, my mum was very cross about it. She said she was going to make some complaint about the way I was treated."

"Still, Chloe, you were a television star for a few minutes."

Daisy suddenly became dreamy-eyed.

"I wish I was a film star living in Hollywood, going to the studio every day, making romantic movies and making millions and millions of dollars. Wouldn't you like that, Chloe?"

"Not really, Daisy, I can see it would suit you because you're very pretty and a good actor, but I'm not – I'd rather live in the middle of the countryside. Then I could find some quiet time to start writing books."

"What sort of books, Chloe?"

"Oh, I don't know yet, maybe stories for children, maybe history books. Anyway, Daisy, I think we should do some work. That's why you came wasn't it?"

"Don't be like that, Chloe. That punctuation stuff is so boring – it's just nice to be with someone of my own age for a bit. It's got so boring at home."

"I think we should look at that work about semicolons; that's what you mentioned the other day."

"Have you thought about being a teacher when you grow up, Chloe? 'Cos you're getting just like one."

Chloe decided not to answer. She could tell that Daisy was trying to get under her skin but she was in no mood to have any kind of quarrel.

"I know," said Daisy brightly. "We'll play cards. I've got some in my bag."

She delved into the bag and came up with a pack of cards with a picture of Seabourne Pier on the front.

"Pairs, we'll play pairs. D'you know how to play that Chloe?"

"Remind me, will you."

Chloe didn't want to appear boring or useless when she was with Daisy, who often played cards with her friends at wet play times. In fact, she thought she might like to be a teacher (just like Mrs Tiler) when she grew up but she couldn't admit that to Daisy.

"First," said Daisy, "you shuffle the pack."

She did that. The cards seemed grubby and well used. For some reason some of them appeared to have what looked like bright red lipstick smeared on the back.

"Then you place them face downward on the floor. What you've got to do is: find pairs, like one seven and another seven. If you pick up two cards that aren't pairs you have to place them face down in the same place. Then, it's the other person's go. If you get a pair you have another go, and then another go until you don't get a pair."

Daisy looked at Chloe solemnly.

"Get it?"

"Got it."

The cards were scattered over the floor and Daisy quickly grabbed two cards, both eights. She then quickly picked up a pair of aces.

Chloe began to be suspicious. Could Daisy be cheating? Finding two pairs so quickly, so easily, couldn't be very likely, could it?

She thought she'd give Daisy one more go, before she said something, when suddenly there was a knock on the door. The girls looked at each other. Answer it? Ignore it? Wait for it to go away?

"Who d'you think that is?" Daisy whispered.

"No idea. Only one way to find out."

Chloe opened the door cautiously. She was aware of a tall

man in a dark blue suit wearing a starched white shirt with a red tie and holding a big, black, leather book. Next to him stood a small boy, probably eight or nine years old, similarly dressed with what looked like a smaller version of the same book. Chloe took a step back and Daisy joined her quickly, taking control.

Chloe was impressed by Daisy's confidence in this strange situation.

"Excuse me," said Daisy defiantly, "what do you think you're doing? There's supposed to be social distancing you know and no one's supposed to be going to other people's houses at the moment, knocking on doors and so on."

The man made a small move as if to enter the flat.

"Don't you dare! Not another step."

Daisy looked round and saw Chloe's mobile phone on the table. She grabbed it and pointed it at the man, rather like a gun.

"Now listen," threatened Daisy, "you are to turn round slowly, taking that little boy with you, go down the stairs, close the front door behind you and clear off!"

Chloe would like to have clapped, although a little bit of her worried that this man might turn really nasty.

He stood his ground.

"Do you know what this book is?" he demanded, lifting it up and pointing it at the girls.

Chloe was pretty certain she knew what it was. They'd been bothered by visitors like this before and her mum had got rid of them very quickly.

Still, Chloe liked giving adults the right answers to questions.

"It's the Bible."

"That's right," said the man. "Well done! And that's why my little son, Timothy, and I have called on you today, to bring you the good news, the really good news in this dark time."

"I'll give you some really bad news in this dark time if you're not careful."

The man and his son and the two girls were stunned, firstly by the sound of this voice, and secondly, by the appearance on the narrow landing outside the door to the flat of a policeman, closely followed by a gorilla.

Daisy's mouth fell open, Chloe was delighted. These were her old friends from the park.

"Right," said the policeman to the man. "I want you to turn round slowly and look at me. Really slowly mind."

The man did so, and suddenly became aware of the gorilla behind the policeman.

He spoke – in a voice rather different from the one he used before.

"Good God, it's a gorilla. What the hell is that doing here?"

The policeman kept his cool.

"Now then, sir, that's not the sort of language I'd expect from a man with a Bible in their hand."

"No, no, of course not, it's just that it's not every day you see a policeman and a gorilla out on the streets of Seabourne together."

The policeman chose to ignore that.

"And, sir," said the policeman, putting great stress on the 'sir', "we don't expect Bible bashers to go around knocking on doors uninvited in the time of lockdown. It is against the law. And if I catch you again, you will be arrested and face a heavy fine, maybe even imprisonment."

The man turned to his son.

"You see, Timothy, just like Saint Paul."

The boy nodded and he and his father tried to make a

dignified exit down the stairs.

The policeman turned his attention to the two girls. He looked at Chloe.

"Where's your mum?"

She prayed to God for help. She hadn't liked the tall man with the Bible but that didn't stop her saying a silent prayer. Her image of God was not at all like Timothy's dad. He was loving and gentle. But Chloe was going to tell a lie, well a fib anyway. But it might be answered. She crossed her fingers behind her back. She remembered Miss Yeats saying that crossing your fingers and touching wood were 'superstitions' and no substitute for proper prayer.

She realised the policeman was waiting for an answer.

"She had to pop out for a moment. She'll be back soon."

The gorilla was standing behind the policeman giving the 'thumbs up' signal.

Suddenly, her mother swept up the stairs and pushed past the gorilla and the policeman and into the flat.

"Can I help you, constable?"

"Are these your daughters, madam?"

She put her arm round Chloe.

"This one is."

The policeman shook his head slowly.

"And the other one?"

"My daughter's friend. Her mum's not well – emergency stations."

Kirsty smiled at the policeman her sweetest smile.

"I'm sure you understand, constable."

He paused.

The gorilla was getting restless. He spoke.

"Wayne, I think it's time for coffee. We'll sit on a bench in the park."

And the gorilla took his thermos flask from his large gorilla pocket and led PC Wayne Davidson down the stairs.

"Time you went as well, Daisy."

"Thanks for helping me with the semicolons, Chloe," lied Daisy, trying to give a very large wink – which failed.

"See you soon, Daisy, I'll let you know where we'll be."

"Lucky you!"

"I hope she thinks so," said Kirsty

"And so do I," thought Chloe.

Chapter Twenty-One
Family Tree

There was something else quite new as well; Mum had decided to join Chloe on Laika's walk before lunch. She said it might be a 'long afternoon" so it was best to tire the dog out, in case she was shut in the flat for a few hours later on.

It had been an eventful walk in the park. Not long after they'd crossed the road, waiting for a big space in the traffic in case Laika was nervous after her scare yesterday, the dog became very jumpy almost immediately after they'd passed through the gates into the park.

"Hello Chloe, Hello Laika, Hello Chloe's Mum."

Chloe and Kirsty turned round to see the gorilla. He appeared to be eating a banana. Laika was not happy; this was a strange being. Chloe thought that her dog would be confused by a creature that looked like an animal but smelt like a human. She wound herself round Chloe's legs.

"Have you met this creature before?" Kirsty asked Chloe a little crossly, but she could see her mum was a little amused.

"She certainly has," said the gorilla. "May I introduce myself, madam. My name is Darren and I'm raising money for the NHS in this time of crisis."

"I take it you're not a real gorilla then, Darren?"

"Very perceptive of you, madam, if I may say so."

"Well, thank you kind sir, you may say so."

Chloe was amazed. She had never seen her mother in such a playful mood before. Who would have thought she'd be joking with a gorilla? This may be one of those days, thought Chloe. What was it Mrs Tiler called them? Red Letter Days, that's what they're called: important days, special days, days you remember all your life. She remembered Mrs Tiler saying that on some very ancient Roman calendar, hundreds of years BC, they'd found important days marked in red.

Kirsty was obviously enjoying her conversation with the gorilla. So, when Chloe found an old, damp, tennis ball on the ground, she decided to risk letting Laika off the lead for the first time. Chloe had never been very good at throwing but she was determined to give this everything she had. She even wiped the fading, yellow ball on her jeans in an effort to make it a bit lighter. She looked into Laika's eyes. Laika appeared to be studying Chloe's face, as if begging her to release the ball so she could chase it. Was this a good idea? Would Laika chase the ball but run off in the opposite direction. Or would she be a 'good dog' and bring the ball back?

"Is that a good idea Chloe?" Her mum's voice sounded shrill from a distance.

Darren was jumping up and down excitedly.

"Let her go, Chloe, let her go!"

So she did. She released Laika from the lead and then panicked because she thought the dog might just race away without bothering about the ball. She prayed. Please God, keep her safe. Fortunately, Laika did seem interested in the ball and her eyes seemed glued to it. Chloe drew her arm back, took a deep breath and… and threw the soggy ball towards the tennis courts. It didn't go very far, in fact, it was what Daisy would have called a 'pathetic' effort. But Laika didn't mind, she seemed born to play this game. She raced across the grass, skidded to a halt, grabbed the ball with her mouth and returned to Chloe, dropping the ball at her feet and wagging her tail. Just like any old dog! Amazing! A red-letter day indeed!

Chloe tried again, a little further this time.

Suddenly, Darren was there, picking up the ball and hurling it up into the blue, sky sending it flying towards the tennis courts. Laika raced excitedly with great speed and, before Chloe could count to twenty, the ball was at her feet. Taking no more chances, Chloe put the dog's lead back on.

Mum joined them. "Hey, that was brilliant!"

She turned to Chloe. "We'd better go home Chloe, important things to do."

Darren bowed.

"Delighted to spend time with you all. But, before you go, I'd like to share a little secret with you. It's about that policeman."

"Really?" said Kirsty. "What about him?"

"Well, I don't think he's a real policeman. I think he's in disguise."

And with that the gorilla was off.

Chloe and her mum, were eating their lunch, a snack lunch of crisps, a cheese sandwich from the supermarket, a choc bar and an apple that looked unnaturally shiny. Chloe didn't want to eat much but her mother was tucking in happily.

"You look happy, Mum."

"I am, very happy."

"Well, I'm nervous, really nervous. Look. My hand's shaking."

"Listen, my love, I've told you. This afternoon is going to be amazing. We're going to do something I've wanted to do for years but it's not been possible. For both of us, life will never be the same again."

"But Mum, that sounds very… very… sort of dramatic. Am I going to have to do something?"

"You will have to be quite brave – there will be some tears, I'm sure, but sometimes they're very good for us. You will have to listen hard and understand that some of the things that have happened would have been too difficult for a young child to deal with. But now we think you're old enough and sensible enough and you have a right to know about your family – exactly who you are and who your father is."

Chloe realised that her mum had said 'we' not 'I', but she decided to leave that alone at the moment. She had a strong feeling that the afternoon would reveal who the 'we' referred to. And she thought she knew who they were.

For a moment, Chloe thought she might start crying already but she brushed aside the single tear that rolled down her cheek and looked again at this new mother of hers.

"Why is all this – whatever it is – coming out now? All in a rush?"

"Because… because… your father is… is…"

Her mother turned to her.

"You'll see, Chloe, you'll soon know everything."

Kirsty stood up and resumed her matter-of-fact voice.

"Time to go, Chloe."

As they were leaving, Chloe turned to look at Laika, who stood there with eyes wide as if pleading with them to come too.

"We'll see you later, Laika. Be good."

The door closed and Chloe just wondered how much her world would have changed by the next time she saw her lovely pet.

"I think you know where we're going, don't you?"

Her mum was walking quite fast and was looking straight

ahead as she asked the question.

"Am I allowed to guess?"

"Certainly."

"My guess, is The Jubilee Hotel."

"Got it in one."

Chloe had never known her mum to walk so quickly. She was finding it hard to keep up but dared her question nevertheless.

"Am I allowed to guess who the 'we' is?"

"The 'we'?" Kirsty was genuinely bewildered.

"When you were talking about me being old enough to know everything, you said that 'we' have decided, not 'I'.

Kirsty thought for a bit.

"You're quite right," she said, "I did. Go on then."

"Well, you're one of the 'we' and the other one is… is… Mr Cooper. It's got to be Mr Cooper.

Kirsty stopped walking for a moment to turn to face Chloe.

"Right again, my love. Got it in one."

And they resumed their quick pace as they drew nearer and nearer to what Chloe was now thinking of as 'the moment of truth'. That was something Mrs Tiler used to say if she was revealing the right answer to a difficult Maths problem or the correct spelling of a difficult word.

"And now children," Mrs Tiler would say. "The moment of truth. The correct answer is…"

Well, Chloe thought, there's no 'correct answer' to what's going to happen next. Just the truth – she hoped and prayed – the whole truth, and nothing but the truth.

They were very near the hotel.

"Now, Chloe, my final words before we go in…"

"Are you sure, Mum, that they'll be final?"

Mother looked at daughter and daughter looked at mother. Kirsty couldn't decide whether Chloe was being cheeky or was just fighting a combination of nerves and excitement.

"My final words, Chloe, are that you will be polite and won't ask too many questions."

"Aren't I always polite? And didn't you tell me to ask questions?"

"I suppose you are, yes. And I did, yes."

"Well then, I'll only ask the questions I need to, politely."

"Fair enough."

No sooner had Kirsty taken out a silver house key to unlock the front door to the hotel, than the door slowly opened as if it was operating itself. But pulling it gradually towards himself was, as Chloe had known it would be, Mr Cooper.

To start with, no one spoke. There was a long silence, partly awkward, partly as if the three characters were just settling themselves into the new roles they were going to play.

Finally, Mr Cooper broke the silence as he gave Kirsty a tender hug.

"My dear," he said. "At last, I have been waiting a long time for this."

Then he turned his attention to Chloe, placing his hands gently on her shoulders and looking into her eyes as he spoke.

"And I do know who you are, my little one. I knew from the first day you walked in here but I couldn't say. As far as I knew, your mother had no idea you'd be coming here so soon with all your questions."

"Please, sir, may I ask a question?"

Mr Cooper laughed a very large laugh at that.

"You must not call me 'sir' Chloe. This is not 'Oliver Twist', you know. You're not asking Mr Bumble for another helping of horrible porridge. Do you know 'Oliver Twist', by the way? And how are you getting on with 'Great Expectations'?"

He stopped suddenly. He realised Kirsty was looking at him and shaking her head.

"Of course, Kirsty, of course. I'm sorry. I'm always going off at a tangent, especially if a book's concerned. I shouldn't be asking you all these questions all at once. We've got to get to know each other a little better before we have a Dickens quiz..."

"Absolutely," interrupted Kirsty, "but first we need to go into the sitting room, sit down and decide one or two important things first. For instance, what are we going to call you?"

"Good question, my dear. Come on then, let's go and sit down."

They went round the reception desk, through the sliding door and into a room which was much bigger than Chloe had expected. There were two sofas and three armchairs, all in a deep green colour, all a little – as her mum would have said – 'a little worse for wear'. But they looked comfortable nevertheless. There were three, small, round tables by each chair with hotel coasters on for drinks, presumably. In the corner was an old-fashioned, dark brown desk with a lid, and four or five narrow drawers. There were several paintings on the walls, mostly of scenes of the sea: old sailing ships, sea birds in flight against grey clouds and rough seas, small figures on a pebbled beach with a setting sun in the distance, a child in a huge swimming costume from a bygone age making a sandcastle beneath a blue parasol. In the corner was a tall, full-length mirror.

Kirsty decided she would take charge of the seating plan. She and Chloe sat on one of the sofas while Mr Cooper faced them, in one of the armchairs.

Mr Cooper looked straight at Chloe.

"I think you wanted to ask me a question, my dear."

"Yes, I do."

"Fire away."

Kirsty was looking anxious but Chloe carried on regardless.

"The other morning, the day we arranged to meet, you weren't here. It was all locked up. Why was that?"

Mr Cooper paused, glancing at Kirsty. Chloe carried on, hardly taking a breath.

"Well, you seem to be a very kind man, not the kind of gentleman to break his word, so I was surprised you weren't here."

Mr Cooper looked at Kirsty.

"You have a remarkable daughter, my dear."

He turned back to Chloe.

"The truth is rather boring, I'm afraid. In the night I woke with the most dreadful toothache. I took some pain-killers but they didn't touch the pain. So, first thing, I started phoning round to find someone who'd treat me. My usual dentist only had an answering machine saying they were closed for the time being – and that was that. Eventually, I found one who was doing emergency treatments and she fitted me in, even though it meant driving to Brighton. By the time I got back, it was too late to do anything. Sorry."

Chloe's mind was racing.

"And that was the day, Mum, you were wearing that very smart suit, wasn't it? Why was that?"

Kirsty glanced at Mr Cooper and smiled. He returned it.

"Well, Chloe, John and I were going to surprise you. I was going to be the receptionist and welcome you as if I'd never seen you before – not sure how that would have worked! John was going to be the manager – well, I suppose that's what he actually is – and then we'd bring you in here and do what we're doing now. Because of the visit to the dentist, I had to come over this morning to sort out some final details. Sorry."

Now it was Chloe who seemed to have taken charge.

"Well, what are we going to call each other?"

"Right, well I'm Kirsty and I'm your mum, and you call me Mum. I'm not keen on this idea where children call their parents by their first names."

"And what does Mr Cooper call you?"

"Well, I call her Kirsty sometimes, but usually something like 'my dear' – because… because… she's very dear to me."

Kirsty thought for a moment that Mr Cooper might cry. He recovered quickly.

"As you must already be beginning to suspect – though you're a clever girl and you may have worked this out already – we are related. Sometimes she calls me something which explains our relationship, sometimes she just calls me 'John'."

"Well," said Chloe, "I shall also just call you John at the moment, and see what happens."

"Very wise, my dear," said John. "There you are, you and your mum are both 'my dear'."

John stood up.

"I'm going to make some tea and find the chocolate cake. In the meantime, you and your mum can be looking at this.

He placed the piece of paper on the table by the sofa.

FAMILY TREE

Anita Dale (1930 -1992)   m   Leslie Dale (1920-1970)
                          (1955)

John Cooper (1942-) m Anita Dale (1930-1992)
                    (1972)

Sid Merry (1956-1997) m Helen (1960-1997)
                    (1983)

Marty Hopper (1980-)   m   Kirsty (1985-)
                    (2008)

Chloe (2009 -)

Chapter Twenty-Two
Unveiling the past

Before the tea and cake appeared, John quickly re-appeared with another copy of the 'Family Tree'.

Kirsty and Chloe sat without speaking with their pieces of paper on their laps. Kirsty picked hers up, looked at it closely and nodded knowingly. Chloe was desperately trying to concentrate and make sense of it all. All she really understood was that she was there at the bottom, born 2008, the last of the Dales, Hoppers, Coopers or whoever they were. She could see her mum and John Cooper, but who were all these others? Why were these two people, Anita and Leslie Dale, at the top.

She began to feel tearful again.

"Oh Mum, it's all too confusing. I'll never understand it."

She hadn't noticed John returning with the tea tray.

"Of course you'll understand it, my dear. Clever girl like you. Most of it's quite straightforward, if a little sad at times. But some of it will need explaining and we'll get started very soon. We'll just have a piece of this delicious chocolate cake to keep us going."

Chloe normally adored chocolate cake but her stomach felt strange, like it sometimes did before a Maths test, or when she stood on the playground while the sports captains picked the netball teams and she knew she would be picked last.

"I don't think I feel like cake," Chloe said quietly.

"Of course, my dear, I quite understand. Maybe later you'll have more of an appetite."

He paused.

"Kirsty, my dear, cake for you?"

"I'm not sure John, perhaps not. I think I'm rather nervous too."

He smiled sympathetically.

"Do you two mind, if I have a piece? Can't resist it I'm afraid. Know it's not good for me, but there you are."

"Don't mind us, John. You enjoy your cake."

And he did, while Kirsty and Chloe continued their study of the Family Tree.

"Right." John rubbed his hands together. "Let's get started."

It was at this point that Kirsty started to giggle. Chloe might have used the word 'laugh' but this was definitely a 'giggle', a schoolgirl sort of thing when you shouldn't really be laughing but you can't help it, even though someone might take it the wrong way. Chloe noticed it too. And then John realised what had happened.

A slice of the delicious chocolate cake had left a huge mark on John's cheek, as if a small child had played with too much mascara, and in trying to rub it away, had spread it all over his hands, which had then strayed to the previously very clean, white shirt he had been wearing.

He was joining in the giggling which had turned to laughter. "You look like a Red Indian on a pretty shaky warpath," said Kirsty.

John stood up and walked over to the mirror in the corner. "Oh dear, I think I look more like Coco the Clown than Big Chief Sitting Bull. I'll go and clean up and change."

"No! Don't do that, John. You looking like that might make us more relaxed. There are some serious things to be said and you looking like that might just help."

"What do you think Chloe?"

"I think you look great, John."

Chloe giggled and settled down. "Okay," said John firmly. "Let's go for it."

Big breath.

"If you look at the top line, you'll see Anita and Leslie Dale. As you can see, they were married in 1955 when I was only thirteen. At that time my father, Michael, ran the hotel and the Dales used to spend their summer holidays here. They had a daughter called Helen who was born in 1960."

Chloe was beginning to see how this chart worked.

"But, John, you married Anita in 1972. How did that work?"

"Well, if you look carefully at the top line, you'll see that Anita's husband, Leslie, sadly died in 1970, very suddenly of a heart attack. Poor Helen was only ten at the time – it was a great shock for both her and her mother. She and Leslie had always loved coming to Seabourne and, as I was looking for someone to help me manage the hotel, Anita and Helen came to live here in the hotel. It worked out very well. Anita was a very good organiser and got on well with the other staff and the guests. As a teenager, I'd always liked her but as time passed, I realised…"

Kirsty helped him out.

"Go on, John, admit it, you fell head over heels in love."

He blushed.

"I did indeed, sounds old-fashioned now perhaps, but that's right Kirsty, head over heels in love."

Chloe was quite good at arithmetic and she'd been studying the dates.

"May I ask you something, John? It's a bit embarrassing, a bit cheeky as well."

She looked at her mother, who grinned and nodded

encouragement.

"Two things, really," said Chloe, gathering her courage. "Firstly, Anita was twelve years older than you. Do you mind me saying that's quite unusual isn't it? I mean, when you married you were thirty and she was forty-two."

John smiled and glanced at Kirsty.

"Good at maths, isn't she?"

Kirsty looked at John.

"Go on, answer the question about the age gap."

"Mmm…"

John scratched his chin making his chocolate make-up look even more bizarre.

"You're still a child, my dear, but one day, when you grow up, you might be lucky enough to really fall in love, like I did."

Chloe felt herself blushing but tried to hide it as John continued.

"If you really, truly love someone, then an age gap of a few years, doesn't really matter. And it never bothered me I can tell you. Anita was a lovely, very attractive woman."

Chloe was trying to work out if her mum would have known Anita.

She realised that she would have, if only as a small child of five or so.

"Yes, Chloe, you're right. I do remember her vaguely. She used to like 'Winnie The Pooh' stories."

Kirsty stopped, suddenly remembering something much darker.

"I vaguely remember a very strange atmosphere in the hotel when Anita died. Obviously, I wasn't aware of everything that was going on, but I remember the curtains in this side of the house were drawn and people went about talking in whispers."

"But," said John sternly, "before my wife died in 1992, something else of a much happier nature had happened in 1983, which you can see on the Family Tree. You remember that romantic postcard, Chloe, written by Sid to Helen in 1992? Well, Sid had met Helen the year before, here in the hotel. And they'd become quite the couple. Sid was in the navy though and was away for long periods at a time, so it was a difficult time for both of them. Helen was a teacher and she'd got a job at a primary school in Guildford and was living in lodgings in the city. Sid could see the Falklands war looming – you'll have to look that up in the history books Chloe – and had come to Seabourne with his old mum to stay here. He was worried the war would come and he'd lose Helen. Hence, the postcard."

Chloe's head was beginning to spin. John was racing ahead at full speed and she was finding it hard to concentrate. She put her head in her hands.

"I'm getting a headache, Mum. It's interesting but it's all too fast. Too many people I don't know or never heard of. Too much to take in all at once. And I can see Marty Hopper, sitting there waiting to appear…"

She started to cry.

"I want to know everything, all at once, but it's too much. My head's bursting."

Her mum hugged her tightly. John wiped his brow with his once white handkerchief. His face took on an even more warlike appearance, which brought giggles to accompany her tears.

John was apologetic.

"Sorry, I've been thoughtless. Just rattled on and on, living my old life again. Haven't done anything like this for years. Sorry."

Kirsty turned her daughter's face towards hers.

"Shall we leave it for another day? Your dad will still be there. We can come back tomorrow – with our suitcases."

"What did you say?" Chloe gulped.

"I said, 'with our suitcases'."

"You mean… you mean… this is where we're going to live from now on?"

"It is."

John got up and smiled a chocolaty smile.

"In the circumstances, I shan't give either of you a hug. I'd better clean myself up. See you tomorrow, nice and early. Say ten o'clock?"

"Ten o'clock," said Chloe and her mother together.

Chapter Twenty-Three
Interlude

Leaving the hotel and making their way towards the main road, Chloe couldn't decide whether what had happened was actually for real. Perhaps it was a dream. She might suddenly wake up and find herself in their sitting room at home, with Daisy counting the pairs and crying triumphantly, 'I've won. I've won. I've got loads more than you!' Despite the emotional turmoil of the last few hours, it certainly wasn't a nightmare.

Neither she nor her mum spoke for the first part of their journey.

Suddenly they heard someone singing close behind them.

"Now, I'm a gorilla

But I ain't gonna scare ya

It's only me in disguise…

No lies, no lies, no lies…" Something, someone, even placed their hairy plastic hands over Chloe's eyes.

She screamed.

"Guess who!"

Chloe didn't have to turn round to guess who it was but she did anyway.

Darren the gorilla was laughing his head off, even managing a fancy cartwheel between his hysterics.

Kirsty was not pleased.

"That's not funny, young man," she shouted angrily. "You nearly scared us to death."

"Bit of an exaggeration, Chloe's Mum. And how do you

know I'm young? Behind this primitive mask I might be an old man. Rather like those bikers you see on the Harley Davidsons – you think they're young tearaways but take off their helmets, and what do you see?"

"I don't know," said Kirsty crossly. "What do you see?"

"Take off their helmets, and what do you see, the crabby old face of an OAP!"

Chloe suddenly felt very tired. She wasn't in the mood for Darren's jolly jokes and restless activity.

"Mum, please. Can we go home, now, straightaway?"

Darren rubbed his eyes as if he was sobbing, overacting as always.

"Sorry ladies, so sorry. I'll see you another time. I might even come and call on you when you move into the hotel."

And with that, and a few more fancy cartwheels, he vanished.

Chloe stared open-mouthed at her mum.

"I can't believe what he just said. How could he possibly know that?"

"I have no idea, my love, absolutely no idea."

Later that evening, Chloe was forcing her fairly small collection of clothes into a relatively small old brown suitcase, plastered with fading sticky labels from ancient Spanish and Greek package holidays.

"Where's Benidorm?" she asked her mum.

"It's in Spain, hundreds of thousands of Brits used to go there every year, for their summer hols."

"Why?"

"It wasn't expensive, it felt exotic, the weather was good, the sea was warm, the drinks were cheap, you could get fish and chips and romance was in the air!"

"I think I've had enough romance for one day," grumbled Chloe.

"You mustn't mind John. He's a lovely man, an old softie really."

Chloe thought for a bit.

"Yes, you're right, I can see that."

Chloe returned to her matter-of-fact serious voice.

"You did very well today, my love. I am sorry it's been rather drawn out but we felt it was the best way, so you'd get the whole picture. And tomorrow, I promise you, you'll learn why it's all coming out now, you'll learn about your dad and then we can move on."

"And us livi…"

"Yes, it is, my love, it's going to be permanent."

Chloe had been desperate to know about her father. But, somehow, this slow unveiling of events was helping her. She had worried that she might find it hard to sleep but she fell into a deep slumber as soon as her bedside light was switched off.

And in that deep slumber, she dreamt again of her father, sitting on the bench, looking out at the grey sea, with the single yacht with the white sail.

He was wearing the same bright blue coat with the collar turned up. But this time there was something different about the dream. The light had changed; instead of mist and shadow there was greater clarity, as if a velvet sun was casting a blessing. The sea had a splash of blue as well as grey. And this time, when she crawled to the bench, she knew there was a man still sitting there, about to turn round and smile at her. And she knew the man was her father and that she would meet him soon.

Chapter Twenty-Four
The letter

Chloe and her mum, were perched in the sitting room, on the edge of their chairs waiting for John to arrive with the letter. The Letter – capital letters – from Marty, Chloe's dad. Over the years she'd thought of lots of names for her father but Marty had not been one of them, but now, this man in prison had written to Chloe in person. She had been told that he had discussed the contents with Kirsty. The letter had now been passed to John who was, as he put it, 'having a quick squint at it' before it was finally delivered to Chloe.

Chloe thought she might explode with the range of emotions shredding her to bits – nerves, excitement, disappointment, tension, stress, delight, horror, happiness, at last, let down... You name it, she'd felt it.

Then, suddenly John was there, handing over a brown envelope, ordinary looking, unsealed. Chloe's hands were shaking.

"Now," said Kirsty, "there are one or two quite important events which we haven't mentioned to you but become clear, if you keep your eyes on the Family Tree as you read the letter. For instance, what happened to my parents, Sid and Helen. But you can always ask questions Chloe. You go and sit in the corner over there and take your time. We're here for you when you want. And, by the way, the answer to a question you asked me some time ago and which I refused to answer is... Miss Merry. My maiden name was Merry. Now off you go."

My Dear Daughter

John and your mum thought this was the best way for me to say hello. That is writing this letter. So, here goes, hello Chloe. I love you and will do my best to make up for all the mistakes I have made, which has made your life, and your Mums, so hard. You have no idea how much I have missed you all these years and felt so sorry for myself and for you and for your Mum for the stupid mess I got myself in. So, may be we start there.

Im not that good with writing words, sorry about that, but your mum tells me you are so that's great. She is very proud of you I know but probably finds it hard to say it sometimes, I don't know. I've never been a great letter writer, prefurred post cards myself, cheap and cheerful, bit like me, if you know what I mean. Oh dear, Chloe, this is not a good start. But, as the farmer said, I must plow on. Always liked a bad joke, just like Sid apparently.

I know that you found that postcard that your Mum's Dad, Sid, sent to your Mum's Mum, Helen, (does that make sense? I hope so, before he went off to that stupid war in the Falklands. Well as you realise, Helen said yes and they got married just before he went off on the boat to the south seas.

I would have liked to have met him because he was, by all accounts, a great bloke. Got a medal for his part in the war. But, I dont know whether you know this bit, but he was never quite the same when he came back. He'd been on a ship which had been struck by the Argies and he nearly drowned. Some sort of shock, I gather, bit shaky sometimes, never really left him. I never met him, nor your Mums mum neither because I didn't meet your Mum until 2005 and they were both dead by then. As you probably know by now. Or may be they haven't got round to that bit yet.

I've seen that Family Tree and you can see they both died in 1997. I say died, killed more likely, in a motorway pileup in the fog. Everyone driving too fast most likely. Struck down in their prime you might say, and your Mum only twelve years old. Tragic. But John was great from the word go and he took your Mum on, cross between step grandad and dad. What a star he is. I know you've only just met him but you'll get to see what a great man he is.

You must of thought about things as you got older. Anybody would. Everyone wants to know about there mum and there dad if they're not about. I know you asked your mum about me sometimes but that she felt she couldn't tell you anything because she was too ashamed. Didn't want a daughter of hers to know the truth. Also, wanted to keep John out of it. Wanted to fight her own way out of trouble, not rely on other people. Though naturaly John would of taken you and your mum earlier if things had been different. And she did keep working at the hotel to make ends meet, though she wanted to hide that from you because you might start asking questions and find the link between the hotel and me.

And now, Chloe, the moment of truth. For the last eight years I've been in prison, different prisons all over the place. The one I'm about to leave is on the Isle Of Wight. But that's not important. There are four really important things;

- *That you know why I went to prison and realise how stupid and selfish I was and show you that you must never do anything like that yourself.*

- *That I feel I have at last been able to learn a lot of things in prison, not just things like being better educated, but learning about myself and how I can become a better person.*

- *That Mum has come round to the idea that I might just have learned something and that we could try to start again as a family.*

• *That I am being released at the end of April and have the chance of a job in Seabourne.*

• *After your Mum and me married we lived in the hotel and John was always giving me jobs to do and to be honest paying me too much for them. I got cross with him and your mum because I'm a proud bloke and wanted to care for my family properly. I got a part time job driving a taxi and one night I met this guy in a pub on the seafront. He said would I take this package he had over to Hastings, he said he'd of taken it himself but he'd lost his licence and needed it doing at once. He offered me £200 in cash. Blimey, I said, what's in it? Gold? He just winked. Is it legal? I asked. What do you think, he said. Of course I knew it wasn't straight, you wouldn't get that kind of money for taking over a box of chocolates. Anyway, I needed the money and said your on. Worked a treat. Quick trip to Hastings. Into a pub. Handed it over. Job done.*

Went to that pub quite often after that. Different blokes each time. Had to find a bloke wearing a badge with a different tree on each time. One bloke told me the tree to look out for next. Learned quite a lot about the shape of trees. Did this five or six times. Money for old rope I thought. Then one night this huge guy with King Kong tattoos offered me £1000 cash for taking a large box. Should of smelt a rat. Big package, load of dosh, must be very dodgy. But I wanted to buy you and your mum something nice so I said yes.

As soon as i opened the door to the pub in Hastings I new something was wrong. It was in darkness at first but suddenly all the lights went on, very bright they were. There were police and dogs everywhere, everyone shouting. I could see one of the blokes I used to deal with being handcuffed and soon the same thing happened to me.

I was caushoned, sent to trial for dealing in dangerous drugs and firearms and sentenced to eight years in nick. I never knew exactly what was in those packages but I wasn't surprised to find out. Just stupid, careless, thoughtless. Should of known it couldn't go on. Silly money for doing something any idiot could of done. So, Chloe, make sure you get a proper job when you grow up, earning a fair wage for a good job well done. That way, you'll have a good life and not waste eight years of it in some stinking prison with other idiots.

• When I was first in prison I was very angry. I kept telling anybody who'd listen, including the governor, that eight years was a crazy sentence for delivring a few parcels. But they said don't be stupid. Them drugs were sold on to children in Hastings and two of them died from taking too much. But how was I to know that I said? Well, you weren't, said the governor, but if you play pass the parcel there's always a risk. But I kept arguing and getting into fights which did me no good. If Id started behaving better sooner than I did I may have got out after four or five years, but no, stupid old me, always had to fight the system.

Then one day the prison chaplain, vicar sort of chap with a dog collar, came to see me in my cell. I was on my own, my cell mate working in the kitchen at that time. I wasn't working anywhere because I'd upset everybody - and that meant no pocket money, no shorter sentence, no fags, locked up in the cell for hours on end. Now, this chaplain bloke, was different. He didn't have a posh voice, he offered me a fag, he said I was to call him Harry and he didn't want to know why I was there - unless I wanted to tell I'm. Which I didn't, not straightaway. We talked about footie and darts and he asked me which team I supported. I told him Portsmouth because lots of the navy blokes were

Pompey men. Then he said did I want to talk about my family. Well I did, because he was nice and quiet and still and he didn't sit there writing things down or looking at his watch. He really listened. As time went by I think he helped me change for the better, not all at once but bit by bit. He brought me football magazines and thrillers to read and then one day he brought in a bible and we read bits about Jesus. Not that I'm Ive suddenly become a great religious man but we did say prayers together and now I do that on my own sometimes. Helps me feel less worried about everything.

3. Then your Mum started coming to see me a bit and gradualy it was as often as she was allowed. She could see I was not so angry. I think she believes that Im a changed man - or trying to be anyway. And last week she told me she'd got the letter from the parole board to say that I'd be coming out very soon. Two reasons. First, I had become a model prisoner and was no longer a danger to the community. I had served my time and had paid my debt. Second. This coronavirus thing had meant that some prisoners were being released a little early to avoid the dangers of overcrowding. She told me she'd hidden herself away in the bathroom and cried and cried because she had not expected this so soon. She wasn't sure whether to be worried or happy. Basically, a bit shocked and confused. We'd talked a lot about whether or not we could start again as a family. She explained that John was moving out of the hotel into a care home nearby (no virus there they say) and that you and she are moving into the hotel. And that when the hotel's up and running again, your Mums going to be in charge. She said that me moving in again with you both would depend on you. If you were happy then we'd give it a go. But I had to meet you two or three times before it could happen. But your mum was very clear that there would be no second chances, any heavy drinking, any criminal stuff, any violense, I'd be out on my ear for good. No second chances.

You see Chloe, I know she's always loved me. She loved me from the start. It's just that she didn't love the man I'd become.

4. So, when I'm released I have to spend a couple of weeks in a hostel checking in with my probation officer - guy who keeps an eye on me when I'm out of nick. During that time I hope to meet you at the hotel with your mum so we can have a chat, see how we get on, and move on from there.

John, bless him, has a friend who runs this taxi firm. He's promised me a job if I want it. No favours mind, Ill ave to work hard, do my share of nights. But that's fine, cos I want to make my own way in a job. Don't want to drive a taxi all my life but its a start.

Hope to see you in May.

I don't deserve you but I love you.

Dad xxx

For a moment, Chloe just sat there, mesmerised, as if in a trance. Then she allowed the pages of the letter to flutter to the floor before bursting into tears, an uncontrollable flood punctuated by sudden intakes of desperate breath. Kirsty stood up uncertainly and then ran across the room to take her daughter in her arms. Then she, too, was howling.

John left the room, leaving them alone, in what emotional state he wasn't really sure.

When he returned twenty minutes later, they were facing one another, and holding hands. The noisy crying had come to an end, to be followed by the occasional sob from Chloe.

John decided to be brave.

"Well, Chloe, how are you feeling?"

Chloe looked at the floor for a minute or two. Finally, she spoke without looking up.

"I… f-feel happy and s-sad at the same time."

"Of course you do, my dear. Totally understandable."

Kirsty stood up.

"No need to say any more, my love."

She changed tone.

"I'm going to take you to your new bedroom – with its own private loo!"

Chapter Twenty-Five
The Start of an Ending

"So you see, Chloe, that's why your Mum wouldn't move to the hotel before."

Chloe and John were sitting on a bench looking at wind-surfers skimming the slightly choppy waves at high speed. Despite the lively breeze, it was pleasantly warm for April and the ice creams they were licking were just the right kind of cold. Chloe felt really comfortable with John, even though she had known him for such a short time. Someone else who felt comfortable with him was Laika who was lying at his feet, stirring occasionally when another dog passed. As John explained, he was in fact Helen's step-father, Kirsty's step-grandfather (if there was such a thing) and, hence, as he put it Chloe's step-great-grandfather. But he pointed out that it would be quite silly if she said, "Good morning step-great-grandfather, and how are you today?"

He said he was very happy with John or just Grandpa, which was what Chloe's mum sometimes called him. Or maybe Chloe had another name she wanted to call him?

By this time Chloe was extremely relaxed with her new ancient relative.

"I think I shall call you John on a day-to-day basis, Grandpa, if I feel in the need of a grandfather at any particular point in time, or step-great-grandfather, if I want to tell you off."

For a moment, Chloe thought she might have gone too far and that this was far too cheeky. To her great relief, John burst out laughing, giving her a little hug as he did so.

"You are such a blessing," he said. "Promise me that you will make me laugh more and more as I grow older and older. Laughter helps old people stay young I think."

"But," said Chloe, "you're not to stay up all night watching those old black and white films you like so much. Edgar Wall Face or something. They won't make you laugh or keep you young."

"Edgar Wallace actually, but you're probably right," he said, "but, my dear, we've gone off on a tangent. I was talking about your lovely mum."

Chloe felt a warm glow sitting there, hearing this lovely old man talking about her mum with such love. She was beginning to see what she had missed all these years. First a grandpa and then... then a dad. Not your ordinary dad perhaps, but her dad, her special dad, her own dad. She was going to see him in a few days' time and she felt excited but beyond nervous at the same time – almost sick to her stomach with happiness and anxiety.

"Your mum is a very strong lady. She was twelve when her parents were killed in that car crash. She was so brave; I'll always remember her standing up, shaking, at their funeral. Her face was so white and her hands trembled but she managed to speak in a clear voice and say how wonderful her mum and dad were and that she would never forget them."

Chloe was about to interrupt but decided to let John continue. Her mum rarely mentioned her past and now she was starting to understand why. She'd occasionally wondered about grandparents but her mum had just said they were all dead and that was that.

John continued, "She felt ashamed that Marty, your dad, had been sent to prison and that it was, what shall we say, like a scar on the family's good name. I tried and tried to make her change her mind about her inheritance, but the stubborn lady that she is, she wouldn't. You see, when her parents were killed in that car crash there was life insurance for Kirsty's benefit, quite a substantial sum. As her guardian, I was responsible for it until she was eighteen, but even when she reached that age, she wouldn't touch it. Left it to me to manage it until she changed her mind. I'm glad to say that she's changed her mind now your dad's coming out, and that will make her – and you – comfortably off."

"What does that mean, Grandpa?" Chloe asked.

"It means you'll have enough money to live on quite happily. She said that she'd be happy to work here as a cleaner in the mornings but that you must never, never find out until Marty was released. She was convinced that he was a thoroughly bad lot and that he would always be getting involved in fights and be shouting at the governor or the prison officers."

"But he can't be such a bad lot if Mum fell in love with him and married him, surely?"

"Well, he wasn't always a 'bad lot' as I put it. Your mum was serving behind the hotel bar when he first came in with a friend, July 2007 I think it was. I'd been taking a dinner order from a couple sitting on bar stools and I could tell immediately that your mum was taken with him. She didn't smile at all the customers like that."

"So, when did he change? When did he become 'a bad lot' as you put it?"

"Gradually Chloe, people often change gradually but in Marty's case, I suppose it happened quite suddenly. They were married in April 2008 and he'd just landed a good apprenticeship with a well-respected firm of electricians. If he worked hard, then after a few years he'd be qualified and able to earn decent money."

Laika stirred. A large Alsatian had stopped and given her the once over sniff. Laika was not happy. The dog was too big. The owner dragged the culprit on its way.

"So what went wrong?"

"The world went wrong, Chloe. Not a virus like today but there was a lot of trouble with investments all over the world – a recession they call it. Marty's boss couldn't afford to keep him on so he had to let him go. Marty was devastated. He drifted towards part time taxi driving – and the rest you know."

"That man in the prison, that vicar person, Harry I think he's called, he had a big effect on my dad, didn't he?"

"He did, he certainly did. Your mum had stopped going to see Marty, but when she finally agreed to see him again, she could see he was changing. And she gradually felt he could be the man she'd married once again. It would be hard for him, and for her – and for you – but she knew she must have one more try at giving Marty a chance."

"Do you pray Grandpa?"

John was startled by Chloe's question. He was quiet for a moment, pondering his answer.

"Well, that's a tough one Chloe. I don't put my hands together and get down on my knees if that's what you mean."

He looked at this new person in his life with great love and respect.

"That's not what you mean, is it?"

"No, it's not. Do you sometimes just ask God, whoever or whatever that is, for something in your head, in your mind – because for there to be someone like that who cares for us all would be so wonderful."

"Well, I'm not sure about this God business, but I certainly do pray, Chloe, if that makes sense. But then, maybe it's too mysterious to make sense. Does that make sense?"

And he laughed his loud laugh again.

"Thank you, Grandpa, that does make sense."

They were quiet again.

"Please will you think of me next week when I meet my dad."

"I will, Chloe, I certainly will."

Chapter Twenty-Six
Home

"You must eat more than that, Chloe. You're going to feel faint if you're not careful."

"Well, I shall be sick if I eat anything else."

Chloe knew that her mum had worried whether this was the best way to arrange for her daughter to meet her dad. Maybe a 'chance meeting' would have been better – or at least something that Chloe had not been expecting at any particular moment.

Still, the arrangements had been made, and Marty would be coming to the hotel in about twenty minutes. He had been living in the hostel for the last ten days or so and would soon be free to leave there and come to live with Kirsty and Chloe in the hotel – as long as everyone was happy.

Tom came in to clear away the dishes, well mostly the uneaten food.

"Not hungry then, Chloe?"

There was something in that voice that reminded Chloe of somebody but she pushed that thought aside. She had other things on her mind.

"No, please take it all away. I don't want to have to look at cold toast and the nasty remains of porridge, thank you very much."

Kirsty raised her eyebrows. Chloe knew why.

"Sorry, Tom, I'm being rude."

"No worries, I understand why."

And then he was gone, quickly and noiselessly as always.

Then there was silence – finally broken by Kirsty.

"Final decision?"

"You go, it will be easier for both of us."

"Final decision?"

"Final decision."

Chloe's mum left almost as quietly as Tom, closing the door almost without a sound.

Chloe had been given a recent photograph of her dad taken on her mum's mobile at the hostel. She'd been given a copy which she looked at again for the hundredth time: an ordinary man sitting at a table behind a plate of unfinished fish and chips, a round thin face with slightly protruding ears, a closely cropped haircut, blue eyes, strong chin, uncertain grin and slightly grubby hands which looked to Chloe as if they were gripping the knife and fork too firmly, as if for support. She asked her mum why she had chosen this view of her father.

"That's your dad, pretty typical I'd say. That's what you're getting."

That response had been hard for Chloe to take. But then perhaps her mum was giving her a dose of reality. She wondered just what she'd been expecting... a prince on horseback?... a gallant soldier back from the wars with a row of medals?... an aging but still handsome pop star?

There was a gentle knock on the door.

Chloe jumped. She hadn't expected that. She'd imagined he would walk in and then... then what? A hug? A picking up and a whirling around as if for a toddler? A gentle kiss on the cheek? A polite 'Well, hello, you must be Chloe...?'

There was a second knock on the door, just a little louder this time.

Chloe knew she must answer it, open the door, let her father in.

He was a little shorter than she'd imagined, but otherwise, much the same as the photo, perhaps even thinner than she'd expected. Then she realised he was trembling, even more nervous than she was. He shuffled in, closed the door and held out his hand – one form of greeting Chloe had not considered – a handshake.

"Hi Chloe," voice shaking as much as hand.

"Hi Dad," voice a little stronger, right hand shaking just as much.

"I've just remembered," said Marty very quietly. "We're not supposed to shake hands. Social distancing and all that."

"That's right," grinned Chloe. "Social distancing and all that."

And they looked at one another and they both laughed.

Chloe suddenly felt calmer, and as her mum had suggested, fell into the role of the little hostess. Kirsty had left two armchairs almost facing one another but at a slight angle, a good two metres apart.

For a moment neither spoke, just looked at the other as if studying a portrait at an art gallery, not rudely or boldly, but searchingly, as if trying to discover the essential truth of a daughter or a father.

As it happened, they both spoke at the same time.

"I've…"

"I've…"

"You go…"

"No, you go…"

It was Dad who eventually started.

"You've no idea, Chloe, how long I've waited for this moment. A moment I thought might never happen. I don't want to make a speech because I'm not so good with words, but I spent a long time locked up with only my thoughts and regrets, eating away at me."

"Dad, Dad," she'd said it, she'd used the word.

Marty shifted in his seat.

Chloe realised she'd prepared this little speech, with the help of her mum and John. But what she said came from her heart, they were her feelings, not someone else's.

"Please, please don't live in the past. I read your letter and it was very honest and beautiful. You are good with words you know, the letter spoke to me, it was a letter from my dad."

She paused, trying to remember what her mum and John had thought she might say. Now she wished they hadn't because this was going well, it didn't need lines that had been learned, as if in a play for a school assembly.

But she said some of them anyway.

"But what's past is past, not totally forgotten, but it's today, a new day, a new start. It's now. You're my dad, I'm your daughter."

She paused.

"Don't you think that's the most wonderful thing?"

They both stood up and stared at each other.

Marty's voice was trembling.

"It is… it is… the most wonderful thing."

Suddenly, there was a knock on the door, quite hard, almost demanding admittance.

"I'll go," said Dad.

He threw the door open as if he knew who would be there. But if he was expecting John and Kirsty, he was wrong. It was a gorilla and a dog.

They scampered in confidently.

"Mr Hopper, we wish you a very good morning. I'm Darren the gorilla and this is Chloe's famous astronaut dog, the lovely Laika! We are delighted you're going to be joining the household."

Laika made straight for Chloe, pleased to be free from this strange animal/person she hadn't yet got quite used to.

Chloe suddenly realised where she'd heard the gorilla's voice before.

"Thanks Tom, see you later."

The gorilla cartwheeled away leaving the door wide open.

Almost immediately, John and Kirsty came through with broad grins on their faces. Marty and his daughter moved towards each other and hugged and hugged.

"Never mind the social distancing," yelled John.

As the people and the dog came together in an unseemly huddle which teetered awkwardly round the room, they took up the cry…

"Never mind the social distancing!"

"Never mind the social distancing!"

Chloe paused for a moment and looked at Laika.

She knew then what she had always known, that dads and daughters, and mums and daughters, and mums and dads, and grandpas and granddaughters, and dogs and their owners, had not been created for social distancing.

"Thank you God," Chloe whispered.

It was at that moment she realised that the gorilla had joined the huddle.

THE END

Printed in Great Britain
by Amazon

14003240R00092